In *Confessions to a Stranger*, Danielle Grandinetti weaves a tale that is at once mysterious, suspenseful, romantic, and inspiring. I was drawn into Adaleigh's story and her admirable strength ... Filled with truths that made me ponder my own life, this novel is a lovely start to what is sure to be a wonderful series!

—Heidi Chiavaroli,
Carol Award-Winning Author of *The Orchard House*

Danielle Grandinetti has crafted a wonderful tale of suspense and romance that will keep you on the edge of your seat. With well-drawn characters authentic to the era, a gripping plot, and a strong message of hope, *Confessions to a Stranger* is a read I recommend!

—Misty M. Beller,
USA Today bestselling author of the Sisters of the Rockies series

Riveting from the first scene, *As Silent as the Night* offers a unique, edge-of-your-seat Christmas read ... A beautiful, gripping, and romantically suspenseful Christmas story you wouldn't be able to put down if you tried.

—Chautona Havig,
Author of *The Stars of New Cheltenham*

A Strike to the Heart is a compelling story. From the very first page, I was immersed into the thrilling action and remained gripped with intrigue until the satisfying ending. The romance escalated right along with the winding plot, creating a layered mystery that is sure to delight readers.

—Rachel Scott McDaniel,
Award-winning author of *The Mobster's Daughter*

A Strike to the Heart is an entertaining story that grabs you on the first page with its intriguing plot, as Grandinetti expertly balances action with the tender stirrings of a romance that will woo your senses until the very end.

—Natalie Walters,
Award-winning author of *Lights Out*

The Italian Musician's Sanctuary

Harbored in Crow's Nest

Confessions to a Stranger

Refuge for the Archaeologist

Escape with the Prodigal

Relying on the Enemy

Sheltered by the Doctor

Investigation of a Journalist (releasing Nov 2024)

Stand Alone Novellas

The Italian Musician's Sanctuary

—Our House on Sycamore Street #1b—

Heart of Beauty (releasing Feb 2025)

—Hearts of the West #11—

For a complete list, visit
daniellegrandinetti.com/danielles-books

The Italian Musician's Sanctuary

romance, history and intrigue at Our
House on Sycamore Street

Danielle Grandinetti

Hearth Spot Press

To Roseanna White,
and my fellow Patrons and Peers

You ladies have blessed me more than words can
express. Thank you for your prayers, wisdom,
and encouragement. Thank you, Roseanna, for
bringing us together. Love you all!

Happy is he that hath the God of Jacob for his help,
whose hope is in the Lord his God ...
Which executeth judgment for the oppressed:
Which giveth food to the hungry ...
The Lord preserveth the strangers;
he relieveth the fatherless and widow:
but the way of the wicked he turneth upside down.

Psalm 146:5-9, KJV

Eden Cove Map

The Our House on Sycamore Street is a multi-author, multi-genre series with authors from around the world. *The Italian Musician's Sanctuary* is written by a second generation Italian-American, so she used US English spelling and her own study of the modern Italian language.

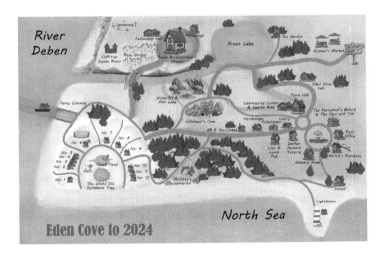

Prologue

Friday, August 21, 1931
San Mirra, Campania, Italia

"*Diavola! Strega brutta!*" The hate-filled words of her neighbors sliced through the night, driving fear deep into Margherita Vicienzo's heart.

Huddled in a ball, she trembled against the cold marble of the church's interior wall. Above her rose a stained glass window depicting Jesus surrounded by the little children. If only her *Salvatore* could physically hold her now. Protect her. He wouldn't cast her away for being ... *inadatta, incapace,* crippled. Perhaps He would even heal her.

1

The shouting outside grew increasingly violent, accompanied by fists pounding against the large wooden doors. The loudest voice reverberated in her ears. "*Tu perisci!*" *You die*.

She curled into a ball, arms wrapped around her satchel, which held her most prized possession. Her nonno's mandolin. She closed her ears to the vitriol and grasped for the music she loved so dearly.

> Iesu, dulcis memoria,
> dans vera cordis gaudia,
> sed super mel et omnia,
> eius dulcis praesentia.

The Latin words of the 12th century hymn floated through her mind, her vocal cords vibrating with the Gregorian chant.

> Jesu, the very thought of Thee,
> with sweetness fills my breast,
> but sweeter far Thy face to see,
> and in Thy presence rest.

Would she see her Salvatore's face today?

Some days, she wished it. Why had God taken her best friend and left Margherita here on earth? Why, when they had both been trapped in the earthquake last summer, had Margherita

2

survived and Maria died? They'd been spending that fateful July day together, singing as they baked, chatting about how they would soon be sisters of the heart because Maria's brother had just proposed to Margherita.

And then the world had shaken beneath their feet, and the buildings collapsed around them. Two days they'd been trapped beneath the rubble. Margherita had watched her friend die, thought for sure she would be next. Then Paulo found them. At first, he gathered Margherita in his arms, kissed her. Declared his love. Until he realized his sister had not survived.

From that moment, the seed of bitterness stole Paulo Sorrentino's love, stole his heart, and turned it as black as the shirt he now wore.

Margherita shivered. He'd pledged his allegiance to Benito Mussolini, to Fascism, to the purging of all that was unfit. Like her. Like the leg that had been crushed the same day as her heart.

"Come, child." The priest's robes swished as he wove between the pews. "We haven't much time."

Margherita could only nod. For months, Padre Benedict had tried to find her refuge while Paulo's hate turned from verbal darts to threats to physical violence. Slowly, like a gangrene, he'd turned her very neighbors against her. Painting her as a stain on their community. Unfit because she was a burden to society. And when she'd survived him burning her house to the ground? He'd declared her a witch, a devil, with unholy powers to survive the flames from which she came.

Padre Benedict helped her stand and tucked her crutches under her arms. Over her shoulder, she hung the strap of her satchel. The few hastily gathered personal effects bumped between her ribs and the bowl of her mandolin. The neck stuck out from the sack, which couldn't be helped.

"I have a friend in *Inghilterra*. A vicar." Padre Benedict urged her toward the baptismal font and the side entrance of their small *chiesa*. "He's found a family who will take you in. I have an associate who will see you out of town. You will be given only the barest of information, for your safety and the safety of the refugees who come after you. But trust these people, *la mia bambina*, they will see you safely off the Continent."

"*Inghilterra?*" Margherita's thoughts swirled, hope and light against hate and darkness.

America as a destination had made the most sense, originally. Margherita knew the Matrone family, who had moved to New York City. Bella, Maria, and Margherita were a trio, a sisterhood, until the earthquake broke them apart. But America had clamped down on Southern and Eastern European immigration, and with Margherita's leg, she didn't qualify for entry. Now she was being smuggled across the Channel into Inghilterra ... England.

"We must hurry." The priest glanced over his shoulder, then ushered her into the baptistry.

Her crutches smacked against the marble floor. Her shoulders ached with tension. Paulo stoked the crowd, his threats growing in volume and violence. The barricaded door wouldn't keep him out much longer. Then what would happen to Padre Benedict? Paulo would burn the church, kill the priest, if he thought he must. His fellow Blackshirts had done no less in other cities across the Kingdom.

"You have sacrificed too much." Perhaps she should give herself up, let Paulo execute her like he thought she deserved. She would see Jesus. What fear could she have of death when she would see His face?

"I have not sacrificed as much as my Lord, *la mia bambina*. One must follow God in the face of evil. May He protect you now."

His words sunk in as he opened the side door to the warm August air. Her priest was defying earthly authority in order to keep one of God's children safe. And, apparently, Padre Benedict had no qualms about sacrificing his life as Jesus sacrificed His. For her. An undeserving cripple who could offer nothing in return.

Margherita took one last look behind her. Though she couldn't see it, she could picture her favorite stained glass window. Jesus calling the little children. This time, He sent a priest in His place. She feared Paulo's hatred wouldn't rest until Margherita had suffered as his sister had. Would he threaten Padre Benedict in order to track her down?

She hesitated. He must have read her thoughts in the starlight, for he said, "Do not be afraid, my child. I do not fear what man can do to me."

Then a dark-clothed farmer she didn't recognize helped her into a wagon, covered her with empty flour sacks. Padre Benedict whispered a prayer of blessing over her. In return, she offered a prayer of protection for him. The wagon lumbered into motion.

"*Ite in pace, la mia bambina.*" Go in peace, my child.

Tears stung Margherita's eyes. Her heart broke as she said goodbye to all she knew.

Suddenly, Padre Benedict turned. Shouted. The wagon lurched, bouncing down the cobblestone street. Faster, faster. Margherita clutched her satchel, and her mandolin, to her thundering chest, then watched in horror as Paulo and the townspeople spewed from inside of the church. Torches in hand. Just before the wagon careened around a corner, she saw Paulo knock Padre Benedict to his knees.

"*Dio, abbi pietà.*" God, have mercy. On Padre Benedict, on her neighbors, on her homeland.

She lowered her head onto her arms, sobs shaking her as the crazed pace of the wagon whisked her into the night. Again, she prayed for Padre Benedict, for all who would risk their lives to save hers—and the others the Blackshirts deemed unfit—in the days ahead.

Dare she hope Paulo would let her disappear into Inghilterra? The thought of bringing danger to the family willing to take her in turned her cold. She couldn't allow one more person to sacrifice for one as unworthy as she.

Determination settled into her marrow. If Paulo found her, she would give herself up. No one else need pay the cost of hate on her behalf.

Chapter One

"**G**RAN?" LUKE FERRYMAN PULLED his head out of the cold brick oven that first day of September as his grandmother entered the bakery kitchen. Usually, she didn't join him for another hour. After he got the wood fire stoked. "What are you doing here so early?"

"I'm taking over for the morning." She snatched her white apron from the hook and deftly tied the strings around her ample middle. The gas lighting cast shadows over her wrinkled features. The sun wouldn't rise for another two hours, pouring unobstructed natural light through the side windows facing the North Sea.

"The fire's not even started yet, Gran. I won't have you hauling in logs." Last time she did, she tripped and nearly broke her arm.

The flash of the lighthouse's white beam illuminated Gran's silver hair. For decades, Grandad and the old curmudgeon who operated the lighthouse had been mucking things up for one another. How it started, Luke didn't know, but rarely did a week go by before one or the other of the old men did something that set the other to pounding on his door. Last week, Old Lennox delayed the egg delivery to the bakery, but fortunately Gran tracked the delivery boy down or no one would have gotten their bread. The week before, Grandad had "forgotten" to wait to ferry their neighbor back to Eden Cove, forcing him to take the more expensive ferry upriver.

If Luke were being honest, things seemed to be escalating between the two. As a boy, he didn't remember these so-called pranks having any financial ramifications. Or maybe that was only because now, being an adult, he was more familiar with responsibility and hardship.

Not his problem. At least at the moment. "Gran?"

She planted fists on her hips. "Don't stand there fussing. I can knead the dough just fine. Get the fire going so you can be on your way."

On his way? This was the only place he needed to be. The Ferryman Bakery had been in the family for generations. Passed from mother to daughter on Gran's side of the family. What began as a massive, open, communal brick oven generations ago was now attached to the back of the bakery kitchen, a stone structure with a clay-tile roof. Grandad added the front room of the bakery for Gran, with its display cases, serving counter, and customer seating. It was the face of the bakery, and where Gran thrived.

"I'm not only good for building a fire, Gran." Luke beat her to the pantry, slinging a sack of flour over his shoulder. They purchased a week's worth at a time from the mill in the next town over. He set the sack on the worktable for her. "What's really going on?"

Gran gathered the raisins and dates she would fold into their signature scones. "The vicar needs the ferry and cannot delay until first light. He's waiting for you."

Another flash of light from the lighthouse, red this time, and it caused a chill to race down Luke's back. Since his father died of a head injury in the Great War, Luke was heir-apparent to the Ferryman ferry legacy, but Grandad showed no signs of retiring. If anything, the older man thumbed his nose at old age. Luke put up no fuss. Though he'd never voiced it aloud, he dreaded the time when the mantle of ferryman would pass to him. He wouldn't admit it, but he preferred the bakery.

Luke paused halfway to the side door on his way to the woodpile out back in order to reload the firewood stash below the large oven mouth. "Gran? Why me?"

"Honestly, dear." Gran gathered the supplies she'd need to make bread dough. Bowl, eggs, salt, yeast. "You're wasting time. Bring in the wood for me, then go on with you. The vicar has an appointment to keep."

Luke studied his gran as another flash of white light brightened the room. The stubborn set of her jaw not only said she would accept nothing short of full obedience—never mind he was a twenty-seven-year-old man—but also that she knew more than she said. About the vicar, about the appointment, and about why Luke needed to ferry the old reverend across the river and not Grandad.

He bottled up his questions, stacked the extra firewood Gran would need to bake bread and pastries for the day, then set out toward the ferry with his kerosene lantern. Ferryman Bakery sat at the far east side of the collection of businesses that circled the fountain between Town Hall and the school. Following the path west, past the chemist's shop, the doctor's clinic, he walked by the livery, fishmonger, butcher, and ironmonger. Other than the nicker of horses, all was quiet.

That's what Luke liked most about being the town baker. It required rising in the wee hours of the morning, before daylight and before the world even thought about stirring. He spent the hour before Gran joined him readying the kitchen for her and communing with God. The ritual of his mornings spoke to his soul. And having it disrupted today unsettled him.

The waning moon hung high in the sky, still large from its peak fullness last week. It cast eerie shadows on the grove of trees to his left. Beyond them, the North Sea crashed against the shore, untamed, even on a calm day such as this. It was also why they didn't operate the ferry in the dark. The small craft crossed the river, too close to the mouth of the sea for it to be safe. Is that why Gran chose Luke to escort the vicar? It must be an urgent matter if it couldn't wait even two more hours.

He hastened his steps, clearing the grove of trees to reveal the twelve homes of Sycamore Street. While the bakery sat at the far side of Eden Cove, Sycamore Street was on the opposite end of town, and the Ferrymans' house was the furthest one of them all, situated in the very corner of the North Sea and the River Deben.

Walter Ferryman, his paternal great-grandfather, the original ferryman, planted the old sycamore after which their street was named. The honor—and pressure—of being a descendent of one of the generational families in Eden Cove weighed on Luke more heavily every year. Mostly because, at least in Eden Cove, he was the last of the Ferrymans. If he didn't marry and have a son, the name would die out. And he hadn't yet found a woman he could love like Grandad loved Gran.

Not that anyone would think the old man was a romantic. Silent, gruff, and more at home on the river than in the bakery Gran loved, the man could hold a grudge as long as the river. Luke preferred flour over water. Smokey ovens and fresh bread over the sea. Not that he would *ever* voice such a blasphemous thing. Luke shuddered at the mere thought.

No. Someday he would take over as ferryman for Grandad. Likely sooner than later. And then, what would happen to the bakery? It had been in Gran's family for generations. If Luke didn't find a wife, have enough progeny, they would have to sell it. If only the Spanish Flu hadn't taken his sister Ginny and their mother, and the war, his father and his uncle.

Luke paused on the path, needing to scrape the bitterness from his heart lest it sour his day. Ever since his confirmation, the day he gave the rest of his life to God, he'd followed the laws, rules, and expectations laid out for him. Love the Lord. Honor his grandparents. Care for his neighbors. Do his civic duty. The part of him that wished to wrap his fingers in dough rather than around an oar would not signify. It was a dream to be laid on the altar of self-sacrifice. For the good of his family, his community.

He only prayed God would not require him to marry for anything less than love.

"Good morning, Luke." Reverend Charles greeted him from the shadows beside the ferry dock. Older than Grandad and as wiry as Luke, the man had been vicar of St. Bartholomew's since before Luke was born. "Might we be on our way? I cannot be late for this appointment."

Luke bit his tongue to keep from asking the nature of this appointment. It wasn't his to know. "Climb aboard, and I'll get us underway."

"You're a good man, Luke." Reverend Charles clapped him on the shoulder with more strength than his frame suggested and lithely clambered into the boat.

Though a newer model than the one Walter Ferryman first used nearly a century ago, the ferry still only held ten passengers, allowing it to be operated by one man. Passengers who had an automobile had to go upriver if they wished to take it across.

Luke hung the lantern on the hook at the stern, tugged on his Macintosh, and freed the moor lines before positioning himself in the bow. Leaving shore, the night mist thickened, casting the moon in an eerie glow. Waves dashed against the boat. His muscles warmed as they worked the oars.

However, the river wasn't his concern. He knew the Deben as well as Grandad. He strained his ears for the sound of another vessel navigating in or out of the North Sea. He'd likely hear it before he saw it, if he saw it before it plowed into them.

"I have spent much time in Romans chapter thirteen of late." Reverend Charles stretched out his legs. "Have you read it?"

"Can't say, Reverend." While Luke read his Bible and prayed faithfully, he wasn't skilled at pairing chapter and verse. "Probably."

"*Let every soul be subject unto the higher powers*, it begins. Paul goes on to explain why we should obey those in authority over us."

A verse he knew well, and lived by. However, Luke stayed quiet, splitting his attention between the reverend and any noise from the water. Everyone in Eden Cove knew Reverend Charles loved to make use of a captive audience to practice a sermon. Not that Luke minded. The older man was a wealth of wisdom, like Gran and Grandad. He just wanted to make sure the vicar—and their boat—made it to the other shore in one piece.

"And yet, the verse directly before it," Reverend Charles continued, clasping his hands in his lap, "the last verse in chapter twelve says that we should *Be not overcome of evil, but overcome evil with good*. How, then, shall we act when the authorities perpetuate evil?"

Luke pulled at the oars and let the conundrum settle over him. He'd never considered such a thing. It had always been his belief that obedience to God, to his grandparents, and those in authority showed his heart for the Lord. Not that he'd ever faced *evil*. Giving up the bakery to become a ferryman in honor of his grandparents and not stealing from his neighbors were obvious dictates to follow.

His thoughts snagged on the phrasing he knew Rev. Charles used on purpose: *perpetuate evil*. His mind often ruminated on a concept while rowing or kneading dough since both actions allowed him to consider a problem from all angles. But rowing did not help him untangle this one, and Reverend Charles had gone unusually quiet.

The slap of water against wood sharpened his focus. They'd reached the center of the river and that sound wasn't waves on *their* boat. There was another one. Close by. Larger, if he wasn't mistaken.

He peered toward the North Sea, trying to discern the vessel's shape so he could begin evasive measures. This was why they didn't run the ferry at night, and, frankly, why they followed the dictates of the law. What did *evil* have to do with anything when the very rules also protected law-abiding citizens?

"For my part," the vicar finally spoke, apparently oblivious to the danger approaching. "I have decided that I must listen to my conscience and show mercy. I hope you will agree because this will do. Stop here."

"Stop?" Luke snapped his head around, lifting his oars out of the water. "There's a boat out there and if we don't get out of the way, we'll be crushed beneath it."

"Ah, but I am expecting the boat." Calm as if they stood in a garden, not a river, the vicar took the lantern and held it aloft. Then he lowered the flame, raised it, lowered it, and twice more. "Hold us steady, Luke."

Luke wasn't sure whether to be annoyed or frustrated, maybe both. Obviously, Gran knew this appointment would occur in the middle of the river. Did Grandad refuse? Was that why Gran didn't provide more information? Smuggling had always been a problem along the coast, but he doubted the vicar would be involved in something illegal. Then again, he'd just sermonized about listening to conscience even if it went against the authorities.

Nope. Luke didn't like this. Didn't like this at all. But what choice did he have? Whisk the vicar back to shore or wait to see what became of this clandestine tête-à-tête?

17

The sound of water slapping a hull grew louder, indicating the other boat moved closer. Now he could no longer get their small ferry boat out of the way in time. Nothing for it then ... he braced for impact, for the crushing of his boat and the rush of icy river water. *Evil*. Luke cast a glance at the rifle Grandad kept tucked along the boards. Just in case.

Like a ghost, a two-masted ship appeared from the fog.

"You Reverend Charles?" a man shouted down to them.

When the vicar acknowledged his identity, the other man tossed a rope to Luke to hold his smaller boat close to the side of the larger one, then unfolded a rope ladder. Luke silently cooperated, hoping this was all legal. It had to be if a man of the cloth—if Gran—was involved.

Above them, a woman appeared. A satchel with three sticks poking out of it hung from her back. She swung herself over the side of the boat, hooked a foot on the top rung of the rope ladder, and froze.

"Go on with you, woman." The man topside shooed her like a fishwife. "Make it quick."

"It's safe." The vicar called up to her. "Come on down."

Luke's instincts fired. He squinted at the woman, gaze narrowed at her feet. She was only standing on one. Each time she tried to lower the second foot beside it, she pulled it back. This wasn't fear. Cajoling wouldn't help her. An injury trapped her on the ladder.

"Hold the rope." Luke shoved it at the vicar, then scrambled up the rope ladder. "I'm climbing up behind you, miss. Just hold on. I won't hurt you."

She clutched the ladder tighter. The last thing they needed was for her to startle and fall into the water. Or worse, strike the ferry below as she fell.

"I'm going to help you down the ladder." He eased himself to the rung below her so that his body created a net around her. She smelled of salt and fish. Had she been smuggled in the ship's hold? Smuggled! Smuggling was illegal. And, what would smuggling and conscience have to do with one another? Wouldn't it be more in keeping with God's statutes to not smuggle?

He'd worry about the legality of whatever this was later. Once this woman was safely on his ferry.

"I'll talk you through each step." He kept his voice calm. "But I will need to lift you by the waist if we're to keep the pressure off your leg."

She gasped, glancing over her shoulder at him. In the moonlight, huge brown eyes met his. Fear, surprise, and gratitude mingled there. It ignited a sense of nobleness in him. Odd, when he'd just been roped into—apparently—smuggling someone into the country.

"I'll see you down safely." He assured her again. "Ready?"

She nodded. He adjusted his hold, right hand gripping a rung above her so that it supported his weight, left arm around her middle. She was small, soft, and curvy ... he shoved the thought aside.

Step by step, they eased down the ladder. She trembled against him, but didn't balk as she trusted him with her life. What type of woman was this? Somehow, both strong and afraid. And what events brought her through the North Sea to the River Deben, to Eden Cove in the wee hours of a September morning? And why had the vicar mentioned *evil*?

Chapter Two

F OR THE SECOND TIME in half an hour, Luke shoved his questions aside as he maneuvered himself and their new passenger into his ferry boat. As soon as he relinquished the ladder, the captain of the other boat hauled it up, waved, and turned his boat into the mist. Luke helped the woman—would he learn her name?—sit beside the vicar, then took up his oars to return them to Eden Cove.

"Are you well, my dear?" Reverend Charles patted her arm. "Such an arduous journey, I'm sure."

"You are the vicar?" Her English was thickly laced with a lilting accent. She wore a dark headscarf that held back a mass of curly black hair and a dark dress covered in a black cloak that made her appear like a black hole in his boat. Present, yet an absent entity. She held her satchel to her stomach, as if it tethered her to life. "You are the friend of Padre Benedict? Is he ... is he ..."

Again, Reverend Charles patted her arm. "I'm sorry, my dear. I do not know. I have not heard from him since he sent word of you."

The woman bowed her head. Who was this Padre Benedict? Her sorrow suggested that she feared he was dead. Exactly what was she escaping?

Luke clenched his jaw tight as he recalled the word used by the vicar. *Evil* ... Never had so many questions swarmed him as they had this morning. He wouldn't ask them, however. Not yet anyway.

"Pardon me." Reverend Charles cleared his throat. "Introductions are in order. My dear, this is Luke Ferryman. You will stay with his grandparents, Dorothy and Henry."

She would? It made sense. Why else would Gran know more about this situation than she said? But wait. An unmarried woman and him under the same roof? Their house wasn't one of those large estates with a bachelor wing. Originally a thatch hut, each generation had added to it over the years as the family grew. Gran made no attempt at hiding her matchmaking efforts, but setting him up like this was beyond anything he imagined she would try.

"Luke?" Reverend Charles regained his attention. "Please meet Margherita Vicienzo. It is necessary for people to believe she is visiting from elsewhere in England. Associates have provided her ... papers."

His gut twisted. Forged papers? He was a law-abiding citizen. So were his grandparents and vicar. How had they gotten wrapped up in human smuggling and forgery? He pulled hard on the oars. Who was this Margherita that they would risk so much for her?

"You, your grandparents, and I," the vicar continued, "are the only ones who can know the truth of how Margherita entered the country. You understand, her life depended on her escape from Italy, and your grandparents have offered her safe refuge."

Margherita's brown eyes met his, pleading that he not cast her aside, that he not betray her.

Could he promise such a thing? Her vulnerability put him in mind of valiant knights of old who risked life and limb to save a damsel in distress. But to go against the law to do so? That wasn't something King Arthur would do. Not that Luke had any desire to be such. His dreams went only so far as being a simple baker who did not engage in such clandestine activities.

He broke eye contact with her and poured his angst into the oars. Was it selfish of him to have doubts about helping this woman? The vicar implied she had fled her home, risked entering a foreign country illegally to escape ... what? Evil? Reverend Charles wouldn't bandy that word about without reason. What monstrosities had Margherita experienced to send her on such a dangerous journey?

A line of violet lightened the distant horizon, and like the hint of morning, realization of Margherita's plight dawned in his soul. Lame in one leg, forced to flee her homeland to a strange country, a strange town, with nothing but the bag she clutched to her stomach. Margherita needed protection, not judgment.

What had Reverend Charles said on the way to meet her boat? They had the choice to obey the governing authorities and deny her safety, or smuggle her into the country and show her God's love, His mercy.

Such was his choice now.

Another pull on the oar brought them into the dock. He leapt from the boat to tie it off. Reverend Charles disembarked with ease, then turned to assist Margherita. She remained seated, indecision bordering on panic tightened her dark features. Compassion softened Luke's heart.

He put a hand on the vicar's shoulder. "Allow me."

The older man stepped aside and Luke straddled the dock and boat. Margherita handed off her satchel, which he passed to the vicar. Then he held out his hand for her. It took her a moment before she grasped it, and he pulled her to standing on her one good leg.

He cocked a grin. "Ready, m'lady?"

She ducked her chin, but the corners of her lips tipped up. It did something to his heart.

Then she squared her shoulders and nodded. Luke wrapped his arm around her waist. The nobleness that struck him the first time he helped her flooded back to him now. It poured strength into his muscles in a way he'd never felt before. With ease, he lifted her and stepped to the dock. The headiness of aiding a damsel in distress muddled him so much that when he set her on her good leg, he didn't release her.

Her arm lay atop his and she tipped her chin up to look at him. "Signore Ferryman?" She blinked several times, as if trying to comprehend his actions. He wished he could, too.

Reverend Charles cleared his throat. "We need to get her to your grandparents' house."

Luke was *not* King Arthur. Honestly.

Embarrassment sprayed him like water from the North Sea, but instead of leaping away from her, he gently put distance between them, assuring she stood balanced before letting go. However, as he made sure the ferry was securely docked, he had the sense of standing on the brink of something big. Something dangerous.

He could deny it. Run from it. Hide behind the safety of his morals. But if Reverend Charles, a godly man he respected, and his grandparents, who had been nothing but law-abiding all their lives, were willing to break the law to aid Margherita ... he couldn't ignore her plight.

She took her satchel from Reverend Charles, and Luke realized two of the three sticks he'd noticed earlier were actually her crutches. She stuck her arms through the satchel's straps, securing it to her back, then fit the crutches under her arms.

Reverend Charles met his gaze over her head, a challenge in his eyes. What would Luke do now?

Thus far, he'd been a relatively passive participant in smuggling Margherita into the country. Put upon. Blindly led to where he had no choice but to help. He could go on, deny knowing anything about her origins, and continue being a model citizen.

Or he could actively become a part in protecting her from whatever sent her fleeing to his section of coastline, which meant knowingly harboring someone who held forged papers and snuck into his country. It didn't sit right with him, that. But more so ... why had Reverend Charles used the word *evil*?

Dawn's faint glow didn't provide enough light to douse the lantern yet. He took it in his left and put himself to Margherita's right, a paltry barrier to the chill wind that whipped up the river from the Sea. They set a slow pace, following the walk that brought them beside the terrace of four homes that made up 2, 3, 4, and 5 Sycamore. He shoved his hands into his trouser pockets, measuring his pace to Margherita beside him.

Reverend Charles struck up a conversation about the various residents of Sycamore Street, but Luke focused instead on the ducks that splashed in the pond under the towering Sycamore tree. Green and full, its canopy served as a beacon, calling all twelve homes of Sycamore Street to its embrace. And the plaque at its base hinted at some Ferryman family lore no one would explain.

He sighed. Luke loved this town, loved this street. It was home.

And he was bringing a smuggled refugee here.

Margherita paused in front of 1 Sycamore Street, the Ferryman house. His house. He watched her reaction, caring more than made sense. Theirs wasn't a stately home. Rather, it was a thatch-roofed cottage with mismatched floors on the edge of the North Sea. No electric and no indoor loo. Would Margherita find that primitive or cozy? And why would it matter to him the opinion of a woman he'd met less than an hour ago?

"*Molto bello*," Margherita whispered, her words snatched away by the wind.

But he'd heard them and he ran them through his mind, searching for what language they could be. Reverend Charles had said she came from Italy. But what did Luke know about languages? He wasn't all that educated, and had never attended university. There was too much work to be done here at home. English and a modicum of French was all he knew. Margherita's words were neither. However, the aw in her tone said the words meant something good, but *bellow* sounded like something Grandad would do when the lighthouse keeper played one of his pranks.

"It means *very beautiful*." Reverend Charles stood behind them, humor in his voice. "I could see your thoughts turning faster than a waterwheel, Luke. Margherita paid your home a compliment."

Chastised, though Luke was pretty sure he had done nothing wrong, he made a sweeping bow to Margherita. "I thank you, m'lady."

Just as the first time he'd called her that, her lips quirked into a small smile. He liked it, liked that he could inspire it, too. Then her gaze caught something behind him and he turned to watch a duck take off from the pond beyond the old sycamore and fly out over the water.

"It is peaceful here." The tremor in her voice had Luke meeting the vicar's gaze over her head once again. He'd stake his livelihood on the fact that Margherita had not experienced peace in recent memory. *Evil* though? That was a strong claim.

She turned to the vicar. "Thank you, *Padre Carlo*. My arrival is not orthodox, I know. I am more grateful than my *Inglese* allows me to express." Her voice cracked, and she ducked.

"Of course, my dear." Reverend Charles smiled benevolently at her. "*Blessed are they that mourn: for they shall be comforted. Blessed are the meek: for they shall inherit the earth.*"

The words of Jesus continued in Luke's mind, *Let your light so shine before men, that they may see your good works, and glorify your Father which is in heaven.* Was that the answer Luke required?

He cleared his throat. "Miss Margherita, my Gran and Grandad, they are a good, godly couple. They will see you well fed and warm. And I ..." He swallowed. English was his first language and yet he could not find the right words either.

She faced him, those luminous eyes of hers reflecting the morning's growing light.

Luke squared his shoulders. He was no Gallahad, just a simple ferryman-baker. But he couldn't get the vicar's words out of his head. This woman wasn't here because she *wanted* to be here. She was fleeing for her life. For now, he knew what God required of him and he'd work out his conscience later.

"I will see to your safety." The waves that crashed against their coast accented his promise. "You can trust me on that."

She sucked in a breath, hope lighting her features.

"It is clear you are fleeing some type of danger." His words picked up steam, as if the building of them over the last hour had reached the boiling point. "I do not need to know what it is, unless it might help me protect you from it. But you are safe here. This is Eden Cove, and it can be that for you—an Eden, a cove—so you can rest, heal, be refreshed. You do not need to fear that you will be mistreated. Be ... betrayed. I will say nothing."

Her eyes dissolved into liquid pools. Lord of Mercy, he'd made her cry. He glanced at her leg, then back at her face. At the sycamore tree, then out to sea. Scrambling for something ... anything to say. Or maybe he'd said too much and should apologize?

Reverend Charles rested a hand on his shoulder. "Perhaps we should go inside."

Of course. He was a dunderhead. "I'm sorry. I should have invited you inside. Grandad is probably grumbling at me from behind the window curtain. I have done this all wrong."

She shook her head so violently, the handkerchief that barely contained her mass of black hair slipped from her crown, leaving her looking even more vulnerable than when she had hung from the rope ladder, unable to move. "No, no, signore. What you have said..." A sob silenced her.

Luke looked to the vicar for help as panic rose in his chest. He could row across a river, knead dough into submission, but women, emotions, tears ... he had no experience with them. Except for Gran, but she was the epitome of British stoicism.

Reverend Charles pursed his lips, as if attempting to understand, even though the man had more information.

Before Luke could urge her inside, or say something worthwhile, she tugged the handkerchief free, her black hair springing every which way. "*Scusa*. I am overcome. My leg ..."

"It pains you?" Luke caught her elbow. What was he thinking, not inviting her in immediately? He'd carry her inside if need be. She was slight. She wouldn't be a burden.

"It does, but it is not that." She sniffed, the strength he'd noted in her earlier slowly returning. "You say I will not be mistreated. It has been a year since I have been free of such a thing. I can hardly imagine it to be true."

Fiery anger burned in his chest. This woman had been mistreated because of her physical ailment? "No more imagining, m'lady. It is time for you to experience it. Now, please let me help you. I will show you our home."

"Grazie, signore." She gave him one of her crutches so she could lean on his arm. "May God bless you."

Somehow, supporting her steps, Luke felt as if He already had. If this was breaking the law, perhaps it wouldn't be so bad.

Chapter Three

T HE PAST YEAR TOLD Margherita to be circumspect, but the weariness of the last weeks left her with no compulsion to fight the security brought by leaning on the arm of Luca—*Luke*, the name was hard to say even in her mind—Ferryman. From hiding behind walls to midnight escapes, the underground kept her ahead of Paulo's pursuit. Having reached her destination, suddenly her strength failed, her leg ached to distraction, and her heart was a bruised mess in her chest.

"Grandad should still be home, but Gran is at the bakery." Luca turned the knob of the aged blue door of No 1 Sycamore Street.

Even in just the hour since Luca had helped her off the rope ladder, she noticed he often worked his jaw, as if he chewed on his thoughts before deciding whether to say them. She suspected he was a man of few words who preferred to think them through before he spoke them. Usually, Margherita spoke first, thought later, but the last months had worn her so completely, she didn't quite know who she was anymore.

However, if she were to play a song to match this Luca Ferryman, she would choose Antonio Vivaldi's "La Tempesta Di Mare." It began with the Allegro's calm tones, but the Largo grew into discordant ones before the cheery Presto resolution. She sensed that underneath Luca's gentle demeanor lay a deep reservoir. Like her enjoyment of a complex piece of music, she wanted to see the full concerto that was Luca Ferryman. But how long would she be able to stay here? Paulo had tracked her out of Italia and throughout Francia—France, she must work on her English. Could he also follow her across the North Sea?

Oh, but she was so tired. Tired of running, of looking over her shoulder, of managing her pain. She allowed Luca to lead her into the dim entry. The brown tile flooring matched her mood. Not dark or tempestuous, both the tile color and her thoughts were muddy, like churned up water. The area opened into a parlor with a faded rug and even more faded furniture. Luca hesitated.

"I heard your grandfather this way." The vicar urged them down the hall.

"But she's a guest." Luca swiped an errant swath of hair from his forehead as he looked again at the parlor. He tucked her second crutch under his arm so he could cover the hand she had wrapped around his biceps. It was a protective gesture that went straight to her heart.

The vicar turned with a lowered brow. "One who will make her home here, Luke."

She'd have to figure out what to call the vicar. Luca called him *Reverend*, but the word felt clumsy on her tongue. And *Charles* was another hard name to say. Why hadn't she begged Bella Matrone to help her with more of this English language before the earthquake stole everything?

Luke pressed his lips together, tightening the muscles along his angular jaw, and squeezed her fingers. For the first time that morning, she really looked at him. He stood over half a foot taller than she. His wavy blonde hair was cut long enough to show the texture. His face was darkened by weathered skin, but no stubble. And muscles angled down from his neck, hinting at the strength that came from rowing.

Paulo also had blonde, wavy hair, thanks to his northern Italian roots. A square jaw and blue eyes. Yet she could not think of two more different men. Even if she couldn't put her finger on what made them so.

She shook the thought away as they followed *Padre Carlo*—it would do for now—toward the back of the house.

Margherita had experienced a variety of homes over the last few weeks, from hovels to estates. She'd heard the term *resistenza* many times, accompanied by a growing anger toward the atrocities Signore Mussolini and his Blackshirts were propagating across the Kingdom. Her heart broke for her people, and she prayed God would protect those, like Padre Benedict, who risked their lives to protect the unfit.

Bowed by the weight of the evil Paulo had succumbed to, she leaned more heavily on Luca. Whether he noticed, she couldn't tell, and the smarting tears betrayed the depth of her gratefulness. Or perhaps she was simply beyond exhaustion. Padre Carlo led them deeper into the house, but instead of going down a couple of steps and into a kitchen, he followed a gruff voice up several steps to a small parlor.

A warm glow came from the lantern on the table, though dawn's first light filtered through a small, curtained window.

"About time you came inside." A leathery older gentleman stood and studied her over the rim of a cup. He had gray hair, a round face, and whiskered jowls. "You the Italian girl?"

Luca's muscles tensed beneath Margherita's tightened grip. "Grandad, I'd like to introduce you to Margherita Vicienzo. Margherita, meet my grandad, Henry Ferryman."

"Welcome to England. Make yourself at home." Signore Ferryman pointed toward a chair, then waved at the other woman in the room. "Our housekeeper, Mrs. Archer. She just brought tea. Vicar, stay for a cuppa?"

Luca coughed, as if his *nonno*'s words surprised him. Did he not expect Signore Ferryman to welcome her? But weren't he and his wife the ones who agreed to house her? Or maybe it had to do with the housekeeper or vicar? She couldn't make the scene harmonize, especially because she immediately liked Signore Ferryman simply because of the twinkle she spotted in his eye.

Signora Archer poured tea for Padre Carlo, who looked over at her as he took the teacup from the housekeeper. "Margherita, would you like a cup of tea?"

She preferred *caffe*. Strong, rich, black coffee. But she also didn't want to be rude to these men who were attempting to welcome her. "*Si*, er, yes. *Per* ... please." This tongue of hers! She was too tired to make the Italiano words stop and the Inglese—*English!*—ones start. She squeezed her eyes shut. Why did she have to leave her home? All that was familiar? Why did Paulo have to hate her so much that she couldn't live a hermit's existence as she'd been doing until he chased her out of the country?

Luca cleared his throat, and she tried to blink her vision clear. She felt the stares of the three men and the housekeeper. Luca tugged her remaining crutch from under her arm and leaned both against the couch, setting her satchel, with her mandolin, on the couch cushion. Bereft, she stood as still as a statue. Did he not realize she couldn't walk without her crutches?

Then, wonders of wonders, he stopped in front of her, compassion pooling in his eyes, and slowly wrapped his arms around her. In full view of his nonno, the vicar, and the housekeeper, no less! She stiffened. What did this mean?

He pressed his palm against the back of her head so that her cheek rested against his chest. "You've been through it. It's okay to cry."

As if the permission uncorked her emotions, a sob hiccuped from her chest.

Luca's arm tightened around her back. Secure. Safe. "Let it out."

And *mamma mia*, did she! The weeping she'd been holding in for weeks poured from her in a cascade. Through it all, Luca held her, as if he were a life vest buoying her through the choppy waters that had sunk her hypothetical boat.

Finally, her crying calmed, leaving her, as impossible as it seemed, more exhausted than before. Wrung out. Dry.

Luca slid his hands to her elbows and eased her onto the couch beside her satchel. She couldn't quite look at him yet. Fortunately, Padre Carlo set a steaming teacup before her, the housekeeper having vanished. If Margherita based the color on how she liked her coffee, the brown tea had just the right amount of cream.

"Off with you, son." Signore Ferryman broke the silence. "You can handle the ferry today. I will stay with Miss Vicienzo."

"But ..." Luca looked from his grandfather to her and back again.

"I will be fine." She wanted to use his name. But would he be offended if she mispronounced it?

She wanted him to know how grateful she was for the care he took, the protection he showed, as if it were his personal responsibility. It hadn't been asked of him, of that she was relatively certain, since it had been his grandparents' plan to welcome her. In fact, it seemed he'd been in the dark about her arrival. Even watching his interaction now that they'd arrived at his home made it seem as if he hadn't known they would have an unexpected guest. Yet he'd comforted her, helped her, when he could have left her to his *nonno* and the vicar.

"All right," Luca said, but he didn't make a move to leave.

"Oh, see if your gran needs help, too." The elder Signore Ferryman clapped Padre Carlo on the shoulder, sloshing the man's tea over the rim of his teacup. "The vicar and I can manage being hosts for the day."

Margherita smothered a smile, the first one in months that truly threatened to erupt. "*Grazie*, Signore Ferryman. Padre ... Carlo. Thank you for your hospitality."

"Least we could do." Signore Ferryman jerked his chin in a nod. The vicar silently agreed.

"And, Luca?" Heat burned her cheeks and she couldn't look him in the eye. Instead, she rested a hand on his forearm. "*Grazie* to you as well. Thank you for helping me."

"You don't need to thank me." He sounded angry. "It's common decency."

She did look up then, wanting him to understand. "It is not as common as you think. Not for someone like me." She rubbed her bad leg. It pained her.

"It should be," Luca muttered. She agreed, but it was not reality.

Signore Ferryman grunted. "The missus left bread and cold meat. Mrs. Archer is bringing it."

"*La cucina*—the kitchen, I know my way to making *il panino*—a sandwich." Margherita shook her head. "I speak English well, but I am tired and the Italian ..."

"Never you mind, girl." Signore Ferryman waved a meaty hand in the air. "Luke, why are you still here?"

She smiled at the younger man who had shown her such kindness, hoping it was enough to give him permission to leave. Because she suspected Luca wouldn't until he was assured she was comfortable. She blinked against the pricking in her eyes. No one had cared for her, looked out for her, like that since the earthquake. And it felt like coming home.

Luca must have read her meaning, because he excused himself, leaving her alone with Signore Ferryman and Padre Carlo. The tea before her was cold now, but she would drink it anyway.

"My wife will show you to your room when she arrives." Signore Ferryman returned to his chair. The front door closed, indicating Luca had left the house. "You have not traveled with much. Tell her what you need and we will try to get it for you."

"I do not need anything." She couldn't impose. Staying here—being *smuggled* here—was enough.

"And your leg." No judgment showed in his gaze, nor compassion either. Simply acknowledgment of fact. It squared her shoulders to answer what he would ask next. "Do you need to see a doctor? I imagine the journey has not been kind to it."

Her jaw dropped. That was not the question she expected. It was more than compassion. It was spoken by someone with personal experience.

Signore Ferryman shrugged. "I was in the British Navy in my youth. Your leg. Do you need anything for it?"

"It was crushed in an earthquake." She glanced between the two men. Signore Ferryman nodded in empathy. Padre Carlo nodded with prior knowledge. Padre Benedict must have told his friend.

"Does it spasm?" Signore Ferryman tented thick fingers.

"Si, si, it does. How did you know?"

Signore Ferryman tipped his head. "You will speak to the missus about this? Her father was a ship surgeon, and she learned from him."

"Your ship's surgeon?" Margherita asked.

The man pinked, and finally a grin won out. "And her mother was Eden Cove's baker."

Oh, she would enjoy staying here with the Ferrymans. *Per favore*, she prayed. Paulo didn't want her anymore, and she had left their country, but she knew him. Hatred and bitterness had blackened his heart.

Ever since he tried to burn her alive in her own home, she'd known he wouldn't stop until he punished her for Maria's death. He considered her a stain on the world, a murderer, a witch who survived the earthquake because of supernatural powers. It was his personal duty to rid the earth of her, the woman he once thought was worthy of marrying him.

"The travel is catching up with you." Padre Carlo cast her a benevolent smile. "Father Benedict only said you needed to escape Italy, not why, but be confident that you're safe now. You can rest."

Margherita stared at him. He might think she was safe, but she knew better. It was merely a matter of time, because Paulo would never let her go.

Chapter Four

NOT UNTIL AFTER THE first official ferry run of the day did Luke have time to check on Gran. The sun hung at midmorning when he slipped through the side door of the bakery and assessed the empty kitchen. The fire had been banked in the oven, but what was unusual were the piles of bowls, pans, and utensils that sat unwashed in the washbasin.

Again, Luke was reminded that this job required more than one person. Or, at least more than one older person. Gran had taught him everything he knew about baking, but she moved slower every year. He hated that he'd left her to make the deliveries this morning on her own. No wonder she hadn't had time to wash the dishes before opening the shop. He should have insisted on Grandad taking the vicar to meet Margherita.

Even if, in hindsight, he was glad to have been the one to deliver her to his grandparents' home.

No use denying that he felt an immediate affinity for Margherita. A feeling he'd need to stow if he didn't want Gran playing matchmaker. Affinity, even affection, was not enough to build a marriage on, especially to someone in the country illegally, no matter the reason. Especially if he wanted a love like his parents had, like Gran and Grandad had, and he wouldn't compromise on that, even if it meant they could keep the bakery in the family for another generation. Better to be a confirmed bachelor and give up the bakery, than make a mistake in marriage. At least, that was his way of thinking.

He schooled his expression so Gran wouldn't suspect any thoughts of romance and pushed into the shop portion of the bakery. Empty. Huh. He stumbled to a halt. Where was Gran? Why weren't there customers? Baked goods filled the display case. He crossed to the front door, finding it locked. He flipped the bolt and propped open the door to allow the crisp September air inside, glad today had not turned rainy.

Returning to the kitchen, he searched for a note or some other sign of where Gran had gone. It appeared she'd collected the day's egg and milk delivery, meaning they hadn't been waylaid by the lighthouse keeper as it had in the past. If she wasn't tracking down those ingredients, could she still be out on delivery? They had several homes and businesses that paid for a daily bread order. It usually took him an hour to make the rounds. Even with Gran's slower pace, she should be back by now.

"Hello?" a female customer's voice came from the shop.

"Coming!" Luke quickly removed his Macintosh, leaving him in only his usual gray vest and white cotton shirt. Then he washed his hands and donned his apron before heading toward the sales counter. "How may I help you today?"

The customer was not an Eden Cove resident, nor a regular. She wore an enormous pink hat with a colorful feather, a pink and white striped dress with a matching jacket, and white gloves. She turned to face him, revealing eyes that sparked with appreciation and red lips that offered a sultry smile. "Why, hello. You're the baker?"

Luke resisted folding his arms. It wasn't uncommon to have female customers attempt to flirt with him. Even covered in flour or damp from the river, the gaze of too many females latched onto the way his shirtsleeves stretched around his biceps when he removed his coat, or the way his shirt buttons strained over his chest beneath his vest. Sure, he could admit to a prick of pride at the appreciation. Rowing and baking required hearty muscles he was proud to have developed. But appreciation was not true love, and he wasn't interested in an imitation.

Nevertheless, this woman's attempt at a seductive look merely set him on edge.

"What can I get you, miss?" He glared at her. She leaned forward as if to offer him a view of her feminine assets. He didn't look.

Her sickly sweet smile said she noticed. "The owner, sir, if you please."

Now he did cross his arms, even if it drew her attention to the bulge of muscle from years of rowing. He wanted the intimidation. "And how do you know I'm not the owner?"

She rose on tiptoes to make a show of scanning him from bare head to his boots. He'd grant her he was dressed more like a ferryman than a baker. Hmm ... ferry ... he hadn't brought her across the Deben, so she must have taken the larger ferry upstream or come from this side of the river.

"Would you like a pastry?" he strained to keep his usual genial customer service while attempting to move her along.

The woman sighed and fished a card out of her clutch. "My name is Alice Walker. I'm here to inquire about purchasing this establishment."

"Purchasing?" Luke stared at the woman. Surely he hadn't heard correctly. "You want to buy the bakery?"

Her condescension chilled him. "Which is why I must speak to the owner."

"The bakery isn't for sale." The words jumped out. Of course, selling the bakery would solve his worries about the future. He could take Grandad's place as ferryman and marry for love whenever God brought the right woman his way. But he couldn't give the bakery to this woman. Even if he wanted to sell, which he very much did not.

She narrowed her eyes. "And how would you know it isn't for sale?"

"Because I am the owner." A small stretching of the truth. Technically, Gran legally owned the bakery, but it would pass to him, or his hypothetical wife, eventually.

"Really?" She didn't believe him, but neither did he like the calculating gleam in her eye. "Everyone has a price. What is yours?"

"Miss Walker, the bakery is not for sale. Now, if you have no interest in buying a pastry, I'd like for you to leave."

"Come now, Mister ... Ferryman?" She let his last name hang in the air. Did she expect him to correct her and thus confirm he was not the owner of Ferryman's Bakery? Or did she want him to confirm her assumption that his name was Ferryman, and thus that he was at least part of the family who owned the bakery? He hated playing these types of games.

Luke scrubbed his face. "What do you want?" And how could he get rid of her?

"I don't take *no* for an answer, Mr. Ferryman, and I want your bakery."

"Why? There are plenty of other towns in southern England. Why this one? Why Eden Cove?"

"I do my research, Mr. Ferryman." She tapped her nails on his counter. "This is a quaint, well-established town. The fact that it's located at the mouth of the Deben means it is strategically located for profitable business. It is also near both a pedestrian ferry and not far from an automobile ferry. I can grow it into a must-see venue."

The woman used a lot of words, but his ears snagged on the phrase *strategically located*. Why would a small town on the corner of the North Sea and Deben River be considered strategic? A slightly larger town would make more sense for a profitable business. Wouldn't it? Luke could attest to the fact that his family required two businesses to stay afloat.

Unless being *strategically located* in a town that had a lighthouse, with an accessible shoreline close to the Continent, was the true reason for desiring this particular business. Plus, the Ferryman Bakery building sat at the very edge of town. Out the back was nothing but open space for several miles.

It brought one thing to mind: smuggling. Something free-trade had shut down decades ago. Except, hadn't he just smuggled a woman into the country?

Luke planted his palms on the counter. "Like I said, the bakery is not for sale."

"Everyone has a price, Mr. Ferryman. What is yours?"

Luke jerked away. "You need to leave." Before Gran showed up and the woman turned her manipulations on his grandmother.

"Tut, tut, Mr. Ferryman." Miss Walker batted her eyelashes. "I'm sure there is *something* that would interest you."

"For you to leave." Would he be forced to remove her bodily from the bakery? He would do it.

She ran her fingers down her throat, obviously trying—again—to draw his gaze to her feminine qualities. Luke marched around the counter, took her by the elbow, and escorted her to the door.

"Please do not return, Miss Walker."

"Come now, Mr. Ferryman." She leaned close. "I think we can reach an agreement."

Again he urged her outside without reply, then slammed the front door in her face. He flipped the lock and retreated to the kitchen just as Gran bustled into the side door. He hurried to close and lock that door behind her. His jaw ached from clenching it so tightly.

"We're locking doors now, Luke?" Gran set her basket on the table, her cheeks rosy from exertion, but she appeared no worse for wear. His worry for her eased, even if his irritation from the last few minutes did not.

"Have you spoken to an Alice Walker?" Luke leaned against the door, fighting to keep the growl from his voice.

"The name is not familiar." Gran removed the coin purse from the basket, set it on the table with a hearty jingle. They'd been paid well today. "Is she someone I should know?"

"Most assuredly not." Luke pushed off the door to help his grandmother unload the basket. "She wants to buy the bakery."

Gran froze, a bucket of blackberries in hand. "The bakery is not for sale."

"As I attempted to tell her." Luke lifted a bucket of raspberries from the basket. This explained his grandmother's late return. "The berries have come into season."

"There is more to gather and I'm looking forward to offering other types of fruit scones, in addition to our usual raisin." Gran handed him a bucket of blackberries. "But back to this woman. She insisted?"

"You have no intention of selling, correct?" He needed to know for sure, no matter his own opinion on the matter. "I told her I owned the bakery so she would not harass you."

"Thank you, Luke." She sighed and the lines on her face deepened. "You need to marry soon, or we will have no choice but to sell the bakery."

His heart twisted. He loved this bakery, and he loved his grandparents. However, he was but one man and could not operate both the ferry and the bakery. Without a partner—either a wife or a business partner who brought money to the bakery—he would be forced to choose.

"You're a good lad." Gran patted his cheek. "Today has reminded me I'm not as young as I used to be."

He hugged her, not liking the frail bones beneath the softness that had meant comfort during his youth. "You're hale and hearty, Gran, and don't you say otherwise."

She laughed, as he hoped, and pushed him away. "Your flattery will get you nowhere. Now, tell me about our visitor. Not the one that has you riled. The one you fetched from the boat. Unless that is why you're more irritable than usual?" Hope lifted her voice.

How to answer in a way that wouldn't give Gran matchmaking ideas. "She is … pleasant." And beautiful and in pain and holding a world of hurt in her heart.

Gran raised a brow.

"And kind." Luke stashed the money from their deliveries in the bank box. They needed to reopen the bakery now that Gran had returned and Miss Walker had left. Yet, he wanted to know … "Why didn't you tell me about her arrival? Why all the subterfuge?"

"Because you have an honest streak as wide as the Deben, Luke." Gran whirled into motion, putting away the rest of the berries and the basket. "I wasn't going to risk the young woman's life based on your conscience. I respect you too much for that."

Why did the words sting, then? "I'm not sure that's a compliment."

Gran stopped in front of him. "Trust me, it is. Your desire to be an upright, honest man fills my heart with gratitude. I've spent too many hours on my knees to think of it any other way."

"And yet you—well, I—smuggled a woman into the country." The disconnect of his God-honoring grandparents doing something illegal boggled. "We're harboring her when we should turn her in to the authorities."

Gran lowered herself onto a stool. "And yet you haven't told the constable she's here, have you?"

Luke shook his head. It hadn't even crossed his mind to do so. He scrubbed his face, then wove his fingers together and rested them on his head, unable to make sense of any of this.

"I'm sorry I had to keep her arrival from you until the last moment. But I knew as soon as you saw her, you would help her."

"Gran."

She raised a finger. "Not because of her looks—how would I know whether or not she's a beauty—but because of your heart. You are both honest and compassionate, Luke. A perfect blend of your parents. But where they could balance one another, you have not found that balance in yourself."

Luke frowned. "I lied to Miss Walker about being the owner. How is that honest?"

"Because you were being compassionate to me. See?"

Did that explain why his insides felt at war?

"Reverend Charles told me what he knew of Margherita's story from his friend, an Italian priest," Gran continued. "The girl was nearly killed in that big earthquake last year and the injury she suffered deemed her a target of the Blackshirts. The vicar asked us if we'd take her in and I couldn't say no. How terrified she must have been to have someone try to kill her."

Luke felt Margherita in his arms again. Felt her sobbing against his chest. He could no sooner turn her in to the authorities than have left her dangling from the rope ladder. "Her leg. It's shorter and weaker than her other. She uses crutches, and I suspect it pains her."

Gran nodded, unsurprised. "If one of my children or grandchildren—if you had been in that position—I would have prayed someone would be brave enough to take you in." Gran's voice cracked.

"You think protecting her is the right decision?" He expected an affirmative answer, but just now, he wanted to hear it.

"Not just the right decision, for my conscience is clear, but a mandate from the Lord. He asks us to welcome the stranger, the hurt, the orphan. Is that not Margherita? The evil she has faced … her life is precious, and I'm willing to sacrifice to protect it."

Luke absorbed his grandmother's words. Obviously, she—and probably Grandad—had talked this over and come to a conclusion. It would take him time to catch up.

"Off with you, now." She waved her apron at him. "Your grandad and the vicar plan to keep Margherita company today. I will sell what goods we can with such an unconventional beginning to the day. Then I will close up early and make sure our visitor is comfortable."

Without disagreement, Luke traded his apron for his Macintosh. The disappointment at leaving the bakery for the ferry was as keen as usual, yet different. It wasn't the smell of freshly baked bread he desired, but the opportunity to tease a smile from Margherita and banish some of her pain.

Before Gran could see any of those thoughts on his face, he hurried out the side door. Perhaps a day's worth of ferry trips wouldn't be so bad after all. It would allow him to work through the strange emotions Margherita had awakened in him.

Frankly, he didn't like the confusion he felt. Perhaps it was better to keep his distance from Margherita, let Gran and Grandad show the compassion she needed.

Then he wouldn't be tempted to comfort her again.

Wednesday, 2 September, 1931
Bella Matrone
Crow's Nest, Wisconsin
United States of America

Dearest Bella,

I am writing in English to practice because God has brought me safely to a new country. How I wish America had been open to me. The stories your letters told of New York City ... I could have hid well there. Paulo would never have found me.

Here in Eden Cove, I look out the front window to eleven other homes looking at me. At my back is the North Sea. Am I trapped here, Bella? If Paulo finds me, will I have an escape?

The Ferryman's grandson—yes, he is handsome, I can hear your question—brought me here on his ferry. I am staying at his grandparents' home. The Ferrymans have been kind to me and my stay has not been unpleasant.

Mamma mia! I should not write these things to you, either, for I know you will worry. But I am alone. I have been alone for so long, I must tell someone my innermost thoughts or I will burst. The Ferrymans have welcomed me, but can I trust them? They are God-fearing people and my presence has them disobeying the law. I am torn about what to do. Do I stay or do I leave, and if I leave, where might I go? Paulo followed me across countries, surely he will find me here.

Ah, how I wish you were here to offer your wisdom. Yet how grateful I am that you were sick that fateful day. That your home did not collapse around you. I cherish our friendship, Bella. I thank God for you every day.

I have another confession. One I'm not sure what to do about. Being left here at the house alone for so long, I explored the Ferrymans' library. I found a family tree, but it is torn so that there are only a few names listed. I made a *riproduzione* (I cannot think of the English word) because when I asked Signore (Henry) Ferryman, Luca's nonno, about it, his face turned ashen and he refused to say a word about it.

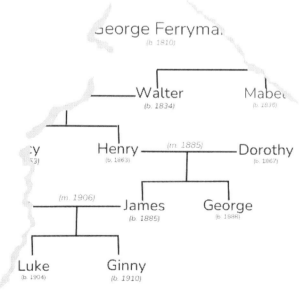

George Ferryman
(b. 1810)

Walter
(b. 1834)

Mabel
(b. 1836)

:y
:3)

Henry ———— (m. 1885) ———— Dorothy
(b. 1863)   (b. 1867)

James   George
(b. 1895)   (b. 1888)

(m. 1906)

Luke   Ginny
(b. 1904)   (b. 1910)

I will enclose the Ferrymans' direction so you will know where to send your letters. However, perhaps do not address the letter to me directly? How is Crow's Nest? I am eager for news of you, il mia amica.

Signore Ferryman is calling me to join him for tea. After asking after the genealogy, I do not wish to make him wait. I will write again soon.

Margherita.

Chapter Five

V OICES PULLED MARGHERITA FROM sleep. She awakened in a dark room, rain pattering against the window. Her muscles tensed. Must she flee?

Memories from the past week flooded back. Her arrival in Eden Cove. Luca's kindness. Signore and Signora Ferryman's hospitality. Padre Carlo's evening visits.

Margherita had stayed in her room mostly, and slept more than she had ever done before. Though unsure of her place, it surprised her that her hosts would leave her alone in their house while they went about their daily activities. Not that she'd been completely idle. She cast a look at her satchel, which protected her mandolin. She'd spent hours strumming it while the house had been quiet.

Yes, the past week had been one of rest, healing, and safety. So why did the voices sound so urgent now?

Margherita swung her legs from under the counterpane, stuck her arms into her robe, and reached for her crutches. The Ferryman house was an odd collection of floors and rooms. On the depressed back part of the ground floor, where her room was tucked off the scullery, or *cucina*, as she called it, there was also a pantry and back door, which led to the outdoor *bagno*, or loo. Up a few stairs and in the front half of the house was the front parlor, dining room, and study. The stairs continued around and up along the other side of her bedroom wall, leading to the family parlor, and then up more to the family bedrooms.

At the entrance to her room, she cracked open the door just enough to allow the muffled sounds to become clear. No heat radiated from the *cucina*, which meant Signora Archer had not arrived to begin breakfast. Just how early was it?

The three voices, each easily identified, must be coming from the family parlor since their sound drifted down the stairs. Rumbly gruffness was the older Signore Ferryman. Warm vibrato was Signora Ferryman. Quiet confidence was the younger Signore Ferryman. Luca. She could still feel the sense of security he provoked when he'd held her the day she arrived. He hadn't gotten within a table-length distance since.

"Gran, don't you realize the implications of having Margherita here?" Earnestness drove Luca's tone.

Margherita shivered. She'd thought he'd welcomed her, despite the distance he kept. Though neither had spoken much to the other the past week. He kept busy helping his grandparents at either the bakery or the ferry. Now that she considered it, perhaps he'd actually been avoiding her.

And why did that make her so sad?

"Of course I do," Signora Ferryman huffed.

"Don't be insolent, young man," Signore Ferryman growled.

Margherita leaned her crutches against the inside bedroom wall, using the doorjamb to balance, and wrapped her robe tighter around her middle, as if it could ward off the chill this conversation caused.

The elder Ferrymans had been incredibly hospitable to her. Signore Ferryman, especially. Which surprised her, seeing he'd sent Luca to fetch her instead of retrieving her himself. The older man enjoyed asking her questions about Italia. He prodded about politics in that gruff way of his, wanting her account of Mussolini and his Blackshirts, as well as Fascism and its growing following throughout Europe.

She knew only what she had experienced, but Signore filled in much. As ferryman, he heard plenty and made it a point to read the newspaper every morning after his wife went to the bakery. They'd shared many a conversation before he donned his Macintosh and left her alone, since by then even Signora Archer, who only aided with early breakfast and supper, had gone.

"I'm being realistic, Grandad." Steps matched Luca's words, so he must be pacing the family parlor. "Margherita is here illegally. If someone finds out, she would be sent back. Based on the fear in her eyes when she arrived, that could be a death sentence."

Margherita stared at the dark, empty hall outside her door, attempting to translate Luca's English words, trying to comprehend. Did he truly not want her here? Or was he trying to protect her? Or simply rid himself of a problem? And why did it matter what he thought?

"Of course we aren't sending her back." Signora Ferryman harrumphed.

She could picture the woman with hands fisted on her hips. She was a large woman who seemed as if she expected to always get her way. Signora Ferryman bustled about whenever she was home, making sure Margherita had all the comforts the older woman could provide. But it meant they had rarely conversed, not like she did with Signore Ferryman.

"The girl is staying right here and helping us in the bakery," Signora Ferryman said. "We'll pay her a wage, provide room and board. We need the help."

Help with the bakery? Margherita often asked to help around the house, but Signora Archer staunchly refused. To be honest, Margherita wasn't sure the woman liked her, and so Margherita stayed out of the middle-aged woman's way.

But now, Margherita wondered ... had the Ferrymans expected Margherita to be a maid, a servant?

Many of the older generations had left Italia before the Great War, headed to America to escape the poverty and challenges of the newly created and somewhat unified Kingdom of Italy. However, their passage was often paid by those who claimed their labor for a set number of years. Is that what the Ferrymans expected of her? Did they not realize she couldn't stand for long on her leg? It was the very reason she could not join Bella Matrone in New York City.

Luca's groan pulled her attention back to the conversation. "It's not that at all, Gran. I know we need help at the bakery, though we cannot afford to pay her—or anyone else—a wage. You know that."

"Tone." Signore Ferryman grumbled.

Luca sighed. "I know it is only a matter of time before I take Grandad's place as ferryman and we might have to sell since I can't run both the ferry and the bakery. But I won't give our business to that Walker woman, no matter how many times she comes by."

"Of course not." Signora Ferryman sounded affronted by the notion.

Who was this Walker person? Was that the name of someone? Or did she walk by the bakery all the time? Margherita leaned her temple against the doorjamb, ruing her lack of English skills.

Maybe Luca could help me? Ha! Not based on this conversation. She would ask Signore Ferryman.

"Nevertheless." Luca's strident tone yanked her back to the conversation happening above her. "I refuse to sacrifice Margherita's safety or risk running amuck of the law. Something needs to change."

Margherita shifted her weight, uneasy. Was she putting undo strain on this family? She was another mouth to feed, one who did nothing but hide in a room. Perhaps she should go up to the parlor and offer ... something ... to alleviate their worry—not that she could do much with her bad leg—but surely she could earn her keep. Or leave. Though where could she go? And why did the thought of leaving pinch her heart?

"It would solve both problems if you married her." Signora Ferryman laid the sentence down like a drum beat and Margherita gasped. After Paulo's love turned to hate, there was no way she'd willingly tie herself to another man. Men changed too easily—even Luca sounded unsure of her—and the very whisper of being trapped in a union with a man who could use her refugee status against her froze her marrow.

"Gran!" Luca's exclamation showed he was as shocked as she. "Tell me that is not why you brought her here. Smuggling a woman into the country to be my wife. That's ... that's ... no!"

"Well, you're not getting any younger, Luke, and you need a wife," Signora Ferryman said, and Margherita could picture the raise of her chin. "Plus, I want great-grandchildren."

"Gran," Luca snapped.

"Do not use that tone with your grandmother, young man," Signore Ferryman barked. "Exploitation also has nothing to do with this."

Margherita shuddered, the chill shaking her entire body.

"I sure hope not. Because Margherita's situation is not about me." A chair scraped the floor and while Luke's voice firmed, it did not rise in anger. "This is about a woman fleeing her home, who came here in need of safety. I won't exploit her, either as an employee or in marriage. It's not right."

Could Margherita believe him? Based on Luke's reaction, using her was not his motivation, but what about Signore and Signora Ferryman? She liked the older man especially, but did he and his wife invite her here out of the goodness of their hearts or because they needed someone to work for them, to marry their grandson? Did the vicar have to beg them to take her in? Promise them her labor if they'd take the risk of housing an illegal refugee? And what if the Ferrymans eventually tired of her or realized she couldn't work like they expected? Margherita couldn't demand a fair wage, let alone fight being sent back to Italia.

Panic squeezed her chest.

Was this uncertainty any better than facing Paulo's hatred? At least with Paulo, she knew if he got his hands on her she would not live. He thought her a witch to have survived the fire he set to kill her. He thought it his duty as her ex-fiancé to rid the world of her evil. Such was the twisted way the Blackshirts thought.

Was England any better? What if the people of Eden Cove turned against her like her own townspeople had? What if they turned against this family for taking her in? The ache in her leg spread up her back to her neck and she clutched the doorframe. She tried to remember what Padre Benedict had told her about God's faithfulness, but only questions came to mind. Why had God kept her alive when Maria died? What purpose did He have for her to remain on Earth? And why bring her here, of all places?

"We won't solve any of this now, and I do not like disagreeing with you." Signora Ferryman sighed. "Where is Mrs. Archer? It is unlike her to be late. Oh well. Luke, get on over to the bakery. I'll bring Margherita over within an hour, and don't fight me on this, young man. She can help me with the dough in the back kitchen if you won't allow her to be seen. But she cannot be kept locked up in the house like a common prisoner."

Margherita should be grateful, but what if she wanted to hide in the house? What if she declined to go with Signora Ferryman? Would she incur the woman's anger?

"Yes, Gran." Luca's footsteps came her way and Margherita tried to scramble back into her room and close the door so he wouldn't realize she'd overheard their conversation. But her crutch caught against the door jamb, and she tumbled sideways.

Her weight landed on her bad leg and she cried out as it buckled beneath her.

Instead of landing on the hard ground as she anticipated, muscular arms caught her. Luca's arms. She remembered their feel from that first day.

"Are you hurt?" His voice rumbled in her ear and she shuddered again, but for a different reason than a moment ago.

"No, no. I ..." Embarrassment washed over her.

Ah, here she was, in her nightgown and robe, the picture of why she was a burden. She couldn't even keep herself from falling! What help could she be in a bakery? What benefit did she offer a community? It was no wonder Paulo and his fellow Blackshirts wanted to eliminate people like her.

She turned her face away from Luke, unable to see the same disgust in his eyes that she'd seen in Paulo's gaze. If only she could crawl back to bed and hide there forever.

"Let's get you on your feet." Luca lifted her and kept hold of her elbows until she had some modicum of balance on her good leg. Then he tucked her crutches under her arms and stepped back.

Confusion and gratitude watered down the embarrassment. How could he sound so ... kind? He neither tried to pity her nor coddle her. He merely returned the tools she used to maintain her self-sufficiency. Margherita ducked her chin. "Grazie. Er, thank you. Lu ... Luca." He'd never corrected her way of saying his name, but it was another strike against her.

Luca shuffled his feet, and her heart clenched. Here it came. The request for her to leave. She believed he didn't wish to send her away, but of course he would. It was illegal for her to be here and she was unable to help as his grandparents needed. If he doubted it, the last moments showed her unreliability clearly. She couldn't risk toppling in their bakery.

He stuffed his hands in his trouser pockets and she realized he had donned neither waistcoat nor jacket. It added an intimacy to the conversation that confused her even more.

Luca cleared his throat. "How much did you hear?"

What should she say? Hide that she'd heard anything? Claim her English wasn't good enough to fully understand? No, she couldn't lie to him. His defense of her to his grandparents, the gentleness with which he'd treated her since they met ... it prompted her to make his unspoken request easier. "I understand, Lu ... Luke ... you do not need to say anything. I will leave before first light. No one will know I was ever here."

She turned to her room, more mindful of her crutches than usual so he would not need to cushion her fall again. Only, he caught her arm, stopping her escape. She raised her gaze to his, finding dismay there.

"You called me Luke. Do you not want to stay here? Because of what you heard?"

Did he like that she called him *Luca*? "You were going to ask me to leave, weren't you?" What else could have caused his discomfort?

"No, I wasn't." He shrugged like a little boy caught playing in the mud. "I was going to ask if perhaps you would walk with me to the bakery. We could talk."

"You were? But what about … everything I overheard?" There, she'd admitted it.

He rocked on his heels. "Maybe instead of making assumptions, we could talk and make a decision together? You and me."

Margherita frowned. "You don't mind being seen with me? Because if you do, that's all right. I understand."

"That has nothing to do with it." Both hands cupped her shoulders as he scrutinized her face in the dim hall. "Your turn. What is this about? This thinking I don't want to be seen with you? Because I've only been looking out for your safety."

Oh. She adjusted her crutches to keep her balance. "My leg. It does not … bother you? That I'm … cripple."

"Bother *me*? Why would …" The emotion that flashed across his face left this staid man with such an expression of agony that she gasped at it. "Oh, Margherita …"

The way he said her name. The sensation wrapped around her like a warm breeze blowing in from the Mediterranean. Like he'd found a beautiful daisy. A daisy, like her name meant when translated from Italian to English. It had been so long since someone saw beyond her deformity.

His right thumb dashed across her cheek. Then he cleared his throat again and stepped back. "Will you be alright walking across town? It's drizzly today, but I carry an umbrella."

Believing his sincerity, and being filled with the desire for someone to see her, to know her, to care. she nodded. "Give me a couple minutes? And I will be ready."

"Sure." He smiled at her and she knew, deep down, that she'd made the right choice.

Experience told her he might not always look at her with the compassion that showed in his eyes now. But while it lasted, she craved it. It cooled the wounds in her soul. Doused the burning ache with honey.

"And Margherita?" He turned back to her, a pink tinge to his cheeks. "Call me Luca."

Chapter Six

NIGHT STILL LAY OVER Eden Cove, allowing the beam from the lighthouse to slice through the foggy darkness. Margherita carefully planted each crutch on the cobbles before she placed her weight on them. While Luca carried a lantern that illuminated well, the walking path was uneven and slippery.

As they strolled, Luca told her about all the places they passed. The twelve homes that made up Sycamore Street, the mix of single and terraced buildings that housed an eclectic mix of inhabitants. Like 6 Sycamore Street, which was owned by a descendent of a former American plantation owner.

A grove of trees provided a barrier against the North Sea for the buildings along the main path. Her nose scrunched as they passed the butcher and livery. Beyond was the town center, a circle of little businesses that, according to Luca, attracted visitors from across the river as much as they provided everyday services for the people of Eden Cove.

Luke opened the side door of the bakery and led her inside, leaving the wet umbrella in a stand by the door. A yeasty scent rushed at her, swamping her with a longing for home. They shed their cloaks and hats, but Margherita shivered in the dampness.

"Here's a stool. Rest while I get the oven fire going." Luke directed her to the wooden table that took up the center of the kitchen. How had he realized her leg ached from even that short of a walk?

Margherita followed his directions and watched him carry in an armload of wood from outside. The brick oven opening was a half-circle at waist height, into which Luca leaned to set the logs deep inside.

As the smoke curled up the chimney, it transported her back to San Mirra, her hometown. The cool floors, the warm smells, the laughter of Maria and Bella as the trio cooked or baked together.

Happy memories morphed into darker ones. The building collapsing around her and Maria as the ground trembled beneath their feet. The crash of stone. The silence as she and Maria were entombed.

Then came the pain. The months of trying to walk again. The derision as neighbors wondered why she lived and Maria did not. Worst of all was the hatred in Paulo's eyes, so vivid it burned like a living fire. Destroying him, her, and everything in its path.

A hot touch on her shoulder caused her to jerk. Luca had set a sack of flour on the table beside two bowls.

"First order of business is making the loaves and rolls that need to rise. But should I take you home instead?" Luca's quiet question was meant to soothe, but her jagged emotions snagged on that last word.

"Home?" She glared at him. "Your home, not mine."

He raised his flour-coated hands in surrender, yet the motion struck her conscience.

"*Mi dispiace*. I am sorry." Why had she lashed out at him? She needed to be the quiet visitor, not the rash foreigner.

Luca's countenance darkened. She'd angered him. Like she'd angered Paulo. What would he do to her now? Away from the protection of his grandparents, would he secure her here while he went for the *polizia*? Her gaze darted to the flames. Would he harm her as Paulo had done?

Words tumbled from her lips. Excuses, she knew, but she had to placate him before he turned on her. She realized she'd lapsed into Italian, but as she tried to wrap her tongue around English words, her insides bubbled like a cauldron. She shook her head, desperation pounding against her chest. If only her leg worked, she could run from here. Instead, she was trapped ... with him.

"Margherita, stop!" Luca's sharp command silenced her. "You're speaking gibberish. If I can't understand you, I can't help you."

"You want to help me?" Bewilderment stalled her. This was not what she expected. Not at all.

"Of course I do." He flung flour from his hand as he waved it, looking more Italian than what she'd heard of the British. Stiff upper lip and all. "Why wouldn't I?"

Her own hand dropped to her thigh, to the leg that was two inches shorter than the other. His comment earlier, about assumptions, came back to her. Is that what she was doing? Yet … "I do not deserve your kindness. I am not supposed to be alive."

His mouth gaped like a fish. Then he slid a stool closer, settled himself on it, fists clenched. One moment the man had been stoking the bakery's oven, the next he had to cater to a useless woman. Why did he show her kindness? She swiped at her eyes. Uncertainty cast her adrift.

Luca gently rested his palm against her cheek, his thumb wiping at her tears. The action should have been forward, even intimate, but instead it calmed her. The last time a man touched her face, Paulo had slapped her. Called her names that replayed now in her head. That had been the official end of their engagement. And the beginning of his mission to end her life.

"I'm sorry I grew frustrated. I only want to understand." Luca pulled back. "Why are you not supposed to be alive?"

Stunned at both the gentleness of his touch and the concern in his tone, she froze. "Because I am *incapace* ... unfit, incapable ... there is no use for me in the world."

"You believe that?"

"My former *fidanzato* ... sorry ... fiancé does." She waved at her leg. "Not only am I not whole, I lived when his sister died."

Luca shook his head. "Let me understand this. The man about to promise to love you for the rest of your days thinks that because you need crutches, because you survived whatever killed his sister, that you should die, too? What madman were you about to marry?"

She turned away from him, more words pouring from her lips as shame heated her insides.

"Margherita." Luca guided her gaze back to his. "English, if you can. Please. There will be time to teach me your language, but I want to help now, not later."

That got her attention. She stared into his blue eyes. "You want to learn my language? You would learn *Italiano*?"

His Adam's apple bobbed. "If you teach me ... *Italiano* ... I will find a way for you to bake that will not hurt your leg. If you want to, that is."

"You would do this for me?"

"If you want."

"I love to bake, Luca." She blinked at the tears that stung her eyes. "That is what Maria and I were doing when the earthquake killed her. I have not baked since."

"Then you don't have to."

"I want to."

A grin spread from his lips to his eyes. "Then we'll find you a way."

Mamma mia! She could kiss him for such kindness!

Her neck heated, and she turned her body toward the table. "Then let us get to work, Signore Luca. What can I do to help you today?"

"Margherita?" He rested his hand on her shoulder.

She raised her gaze, and he studied her in return. When she saw no judgment, no lingering anger, she relaxed.

So did he. "Good. I hated seeing the torture in your eyes. It was ... it seemed ... well, it looked like it could consume you like the fire within my oven."

"You have a bit of the *artista* in you." Which he kept well hidden. But it was there. Deep inside.

"Artist? I don't know about that." He tapped the table. "I also don't know what the vicar or my grandparents were thinking, bringing an illegal refugee here. What I was thinking, inviting you here alone with me ... highly improper. But ... I'm glad they—I—did."

Margherita ducked her head, not wanting him to see that his words both pleased and embarrassed her.

Luca cleared his throat. "Let's have you make our signature scone recipe, and I'll work on the rest."

"Signature scone? Are you sure?" That sounded like a lot of responsibility.

"It's rather simple. I'll gather the ingredients." Luca set before her the bowl he'd originally brought to the table and handed her a measuring cup. "Sift in four cups of flour, if you will."

Margherita gave a definitive nod and followed his direction. Luca set sugar, salt, and a bowl of dried fruit beside the bag of flour.

"Now, this little ingredient is a miracle." He waggled a can of baking powder. "Can you imagine what it was like before?"

"Having to mix sour milk and cornstarch?" Margherita could still remember her own nonna telling stories about the challenges of baking fluffy bread.

"Cornstarch is still helpful, though." He poured a bit of sugar into pestle, then added some cornstarch before pulverizing it with the mortar. "Adding it to ground sugar makes confectioner's sugar."

Margherita mixed the dry ingredients together. "What makes this recipe signature?"

"We add in various types of dried fruit." He showed her the bowl of raisins before dumping them into her bowl. "And vanilla."

"Vanilla?"

He nodded, showing her the brown bottle of extract. "It adds a delightful flavor. But that's not the only special ingredient."

She continued to stir, enjoying this side of Luca. In the week she'd known him, he'd spoken only when necessary and seemed the epitome of composure, only giving hints at the emotion underneath that level exterior. Seeing the animation baking brought out in him made her want to see more. Perhaps if she did, she wouldn't feel the need to tamp down on her own expressive tendencies.

"Oops, forgot the cream." A few long strides brought Luca to the icebox. He returned with a glass jug of milk. No, cream. Its thickness was clear as he poured a portion into another glass container that held several cups. "When you're ready, pour this in, but only stir until the flour is saturated. Over-stirring is death to a good scone."

Ah, she liked this side of him!

"Back to that other special ingredient. Oranges."

"Oranges?" Margherita paused with the pitcher of cream midair.

"It's getting expensive these last couple years, I admit, and we've had to switch to Seville oranges—what we use to make marmalade. But it's worth it for this recipe."

She poured the cream into the flour mixture. "South of where I live ... lived ... in Italia, they grow oranges. *Arancia rossa*, they are called, or red orange."

"Ar-an-cha ro-so?"

Margherita's shoulders bounced in a laugh. She rolled the *R*. "Ro-*sa*."

Luca grinned. "*Rossa*. My first Italian word. It looks like you've combined the ingredients well enough."

Margherita stopped immediately, not wanting to ruin the recipe.

Luca sprinkled flour on the table. "Set the dough on the flour and knead it a couple of times. That's it. Now, separate the dough into rounds of, oh, yea big." He showed the size with his hands.

She followed his directions as he sliced an orange in half, the tangy scent filling the air. He poured the crushed sugar mixture into another bowl, then squeezed the juice of the orange into it.

"This part is not exact." Luca dipped a spoon into the mixture and tasted it. "Especially now that we have to use the more bitter oranges, it's important to get the right ratio of sugar to juice."

Margherita smiled. She cut the circles of dough into quarters, as he directed, and she couldn't help comparing him to Paulo once more. The staid artist versus the explosive fascist. She'd thought she liked Paulo's expressive ways. They had wonderful debates, though in hindsight, she now realized he had always tried to change her mind, never allowing her to change his. Luca, however, defied his usual aplomb with the creativity she'd witnessed today.

For several minutes, they worked in comfortable silence, side-by-side. Peace settled over her. Luca set aside his orange-sugar mixture, checked the oven temperature, then slid her quartered rounds onto a wooden paddle to place in the oven.

Just as he finished, the back door banged open. Margherita jumped with a squeal. Luca brandished the paddle like a weapon.

"Blimey!" Signora Ferryman pulled up short. "Put that away, Luke. Who did you think would come through the door at this hour?"

Luca reddened and set the paddle beside the oven.

Signora Ferryman scanned the room, and her eyebrows lowered as her gaze bounced between her grandson and Margherita. "You have been less than efficient today, Luke Ferryman. Do I need to be concerned?"

Was his grandmother questioning Luca's honor? "Signora, Luca merely taught me to make your scones. They are in the oven now."

"We do not begin the morning with the scones." Signora planted fists on her hips as she stared down her grandson. "We begin with rolls and loaves. The delivery items, which will now be late."

Luca bowed his head and his lack of self-defense irritated Margherita. How dare his nonna berate him for helping Margherita as the older woman had demanded? "You are the one who wished me here, Signora. I am here and Luca is making the best of the situation. Or perhaps you should have been here from the beginning?"

Signora Ferryman gasped. Luca's gaze shot to hers, his eyes wide. And Margherita realized what she said. But she wasn't sorry. It wasn't fair of his grandmother.

Margherita raised her chin. "I heard you this morning, Signora. I heard you want Luca to marry me and for me to work in your bakery. Luca has been nothing but kind to me and if my words mean I must find a different refuge, then so be it." She held her breath, waiting for the judgment she'd called down on herself.

But Luca stepped between them. "I did get distracted, Gran. I'm sorry I did not begin with the rolls. And Margherita, there is no need for you to find somewhere else to … stay. This has been entirely my fault."

Signora Ferryman pressed her lips together, but Margherita could only blink. Never had she heard a man apologize before. And it made her appreciate Luca Ferryman all the more.

"I'm glad to hear that, Luke." Signora Ferryman deflated. "After our conversation this morning, I worried what my rule-following grandson would do. I admit I had myself worked up on the way here. Are you quite alright, Margherita?"

Margherita nodded. She sensed that this morning's emotional eruptions had been building all week. Now that the words had been expressed, would they settle into a normal pattern of life? But what was normal? Margherita's very presence was like a sliver under the skin. Until she was removed, tensions would only fester again.

She prized harmony. Discordant notes were her least favorite within a piece of music. To be that chord here among the Ferryman family was its own thorn of doubt under her skin.

Was Paulo right? Was she a destroyer of families? That was the last thing she wanted to do to Luca's family. She cared too much for them already.

Wednesday, 9 September, 1931
Bella Matrone
Crow's Nest, Wisconsin
United States of America

Dearest Bella,

This morning, I left the Ferryman home on Sycamore Street for the first time since I arrived. Do not fear, I was not alone. Luca escorted me to the bakery to help his grandmother.

If not for Paulo, I might have enjoyed being outside. However, leaving their house to walk to their bakery, I felt on display, even in the dark early morning with a powerful protector beside me. The lighthouse flashed like a spotlight. I was sure Paulo would leap from the shadows. Of course he did not, but it shook me more than I wished to show Luca.

He taught me to make his family's scone recipe, and he wants to learn Italian. Can you believe it? He is a kind man, Bella. Still, after this past year, I am afraid. I pray he is nothing like Paulo. I don't think so, but how can I trust him? Do you have advice?

What of you? The last I read before I had to flee our home said you would join your brother in Crow's Nest. What an odd name for a town. Crows are horrible birds. I hope the place is not like them and you are happy there. I long to hear your stories.

Signora Ferryman has returned from her bakery, so I must say *arrivederci*.

Ah, *la mia amica*, I miss you.

Margherita

Chapter Seven

Luke detoured to the North Sea on his way home from morning deliveries. The sun rose over the gray, churning water. Red and purple streaked the low clouds like a bruise in the sky. More rain would fall before the day ended.

It'd been ten days since his first morning with Margherita in the bakery, and Luke looked forward to what had become their routine. Luke and Margherita would walk to the bakery after a cuppa with Gran and Grandad, Gran following shortly. By the time she arrived, Luke and Margherita had the oven hot, the rolls and scones ready for baking, and the loaves rising. Then he would escort Margherita back to the house on his way to deliver the baked goods.

While she never mentioned that first day, Gran's reaction hadn't been far from Luke's thoughts. The juxtaposition of her sending Luke and Margherita alone to the bakery, and yet keeping a chaperone's eye on them once she arrived, spoke of meddling and protection. Luke wasn't sure he approved of the mix.

However, he kept quiet because he enjoyed his conversations with Margherita. She was very much his opposite, and so full of life despite the circumstances that sent her into flight.

He hated to think that someone wanted her dead. And that thought had brought him to the sea today. He needed a moment to think … without Margherita's intelligent eyes watching him, or Gran's confusing matchmaking, or even Grandad's expectation for the future.

Luke tossed a stone into the water. It'd been nearly three weeks since Margherita arrived in Eden Cove. So far, no one in their small town had mentioned her presence, so they had succeeded in keeping her hidden. Was she also sufficiently removed from the man—Paulo—who wanted her dead so that it would be safe to introduce her to others in town? Or was Luke being selfish, desiring her company more often than just in the predawn mornings?

Therein lay the crux of the matter. He threw another rock. Harder this time. He hated that Gran's matchmaking muddled what should be straightforward. He liked Margherita, but it was too soon to even consider offering more than friendship. Margherita was here illegally. She was hiding, a refugee from her homeland. Suggesting more wasn't right. Was it?

He'd always considered himself to be a law-abiding citizen, yet the last month had seen him smuggle a human into his country and harbor an illegal visitor. They had a plan in place if the constable found out about Margherita, but even that cover was essentially a lie.

How were those actions honoring God?

The alternative was handing Margherita over to the authorities. They would send her back to Italy. Back to the danger that threatened her life. To the man who would kill her.

How was that any more honorable than shielding her with a lie?

More baffled than ever, Luke cut through the grove of trees to the bridge across the canal connecting the River Deben to Great Lake. Castle on the Hill, which once belonged to the Brandon family, rose to his left, high on the cliff overlooking the river. The castle and the family who once lived there had some connection to great-grandad Walter Ferryman, but no one spoke of it. The castle itself had been through a couple disasters before Luke was born and was now deserted and in disrepair.

The path curved past a rose garden with a few late blooms still holding on despite the coming winter. A picture of Margherita … beautiful in the face of that which could destroy her.

Luke shook his head to clear it. He needed godly wisdom, not fanciful thoughts.

Reverend Charles could often be found tending the garden. Not today, however. So Luke made his way up to St.

Bartholomew's. The stone building, with large stained glass windows and a tall steeple, had stood since the founding of Eden Cove. A beacon to the soul as the lighthouse was to passing ships.

Luke pushed open the heavy wooden door and stepped into the cool interior. It took only a moment to spot the vicar in his black shirt and trousers at the front of the church sanctuary.

"Luke!" The older man beckoned him down the aisle. "A pleasure to see you."

They exchanged the usual greetings as Luke made his way forward. The weather, his grandparents' health, today's bakery special ... all circling around the obvious like boxers in a ring.

Reverend Charles clasped his hands at his waist. "And how is our guest faring?"

And there it was. Leave it to the vicar to home in on the truth.

"She is partly the reason I'm here." Luke sat in the first pew and rested his elbows on his knees. "I'm worried about how long she's being sequestered away. It isn't good for a person."

He'd work up to his real questions. Eventually. Maybe. Probably.

"Hmm." Reverend Charles sat beside him. "You think she is safe to interact with the community?"

"I don't know." It felt like there was much he didn't know. It wouldn't bother him so much if it didn't feel like the very foundation of all that was right was shifting beneath his feet.

"You are concerned."

"I've been concerned since the moment I helped her down the rope ladder." The words shot out of his mouth with a healthy dose of censure.

To speak so to a man of God! A man he respected. How addled was he?

Luke dropped his face into his hands. "I'm sorry, Reverend Charles."

The man's hand came down on his shoulder. "I am not easily offended, nor is God. Speak honestly. Your thoughts are safe here."

Not looking at the man, Luke's inner turmoil poured out. His concern over Margherita's safety. How being hidden away could affect her. His enjoyment of her company. Gran's matchmaking ideas. The pressure he felt to marry. The thought that the first woman to catch his attention was an illegal refugee running from her former fiancé.

"Are you asking for guidance?" Reverend Charles asked once Luke had expended more words than he usually spoke in a day.

"Maybe." The thought of criticism had him wishing he'd kept his mouth shut.

"Seems to me you are looking more for affirmation than advice."

Luke raised his head. "Is that wrong? What if I'm ... well, afraid that what I want isn't what is wise or right or what God would have for me?" *And Margherita.*

"You ask a wonderful question, Luke." The vicar pressed steepled fingers against his mouth. Was he praying for wisdom to lead an errant sheep? "Have you asked Margherita about her view of God?"

"What?" Luke sat up, the out-of-nowhere question scrambling his thoughts.

"First, she is Catholic, as most of her countrymen are. Her priest, my friend Father Benedict, is a staunch supporter of the Roman Church. He and I have exchanged many missives about the difference between his church and the Church of England."

"What does that have to do with housing her illegally?"

The vicar cast him a side eye. "You can't marry her unless she joins our church."

Luke sputtered. "Who said anything about me marrying her?"

"Secondly, she has seen more evil than most, and experienced more. If you are as concerned for her well-being as you claim, you will check on her soul."

"I hear you. I do. But that doesn't answer my question. How is it honorable to smuggle in an illegal refugee, then lie about it if we're caught?"

"How is it honorable to knowingly send an innocent person to her death?"

"Exactly!" Luke jumped to his feet. "If I help her, will I lose my soul?"

"Are you willing to do that?"

The question hammered Luke. Yes, was his immediate answer.

"Read about the midwives who saved Israelite babies in Egypt. And Rahab who saved the two spies. And in Jesus's own words when He said to welcome the stranger and in doing so you welcome Him."

Luke nodded, knowing he would do just that. Had to.

"Good. Talk to Margherita." Reverend Charles winked. "Then return, and we'll talk more."

Left with a mission and a place to search for answers, Luke made his way back to the bakery. Gran held court behind the counter, talking with customers as they ordered. The line stretched to the front door, so Luke donned his apron and came to her aid. Five customers in and he wished he'd stayed at St. Bartholomew's a few minutes longer.

"Hello, Mr. Ferryman." Alice Walker slowly lifted her lips into a smile, as if that would seduce him. Ha. He preferred bright, astute eyes to a false smile.

I do? There was one person who had eyes like that. Margherita.

"What may I get you today?" He purposefully avoided using Miss Walker's name so she wouldn't get the idea that he remembered her.

"Come now, Mr. Ferryman. I'd like to speak to you about my offer."

He certainly didn't want Miss Walker to realize Gran had more say in a decision to sell the bakery than he did. The woman would hound Gran, he had no doubt. Willing to take the brunt of Miss Walker's forwardness to spare his grandmother, he beckoned the woman to the kitchen. But he didn't offer her a chair.

Miss Walker huffed. "I take it you're not willing to sell."

"You would be correct." Luke folded his arms. Heat still radiated from the oven, though the wood had burned down to smoldering ashes.

"I urge you to reconsider." She glided a gloved finger along the worn surface of the table. "I will make it worth your while."

Luke contained a shudder. He couldn't decide if Miss Walker thought she was flirting with or threatening him. Neither was an option he liked. He allowed an uncomfortable silence to build. What could he say that he hadn't already?

She sighed and removed several papers from the bag that hung from her arm. "Since it seems we are at an impasse, here is the contract. Sign it, Mr. Ferryman."

"Why won't you take me at my word?" He pressed his palms onto the table. "The bakery is *not* for sale."

"That would be a mistake." She slid the papers toward him. "Sign it."

"Why? What is the benefit for me?" And why did she want this building so much? Why was it such a *strategic location* for her?

She adjusted her bag on her arm. "I'll return next week so we can—"

Luke snatched the contract and tore it in two. "That's my answer, Miss Walker. Allow me to escort you out." He held his arm toward the side doorway. No way would he let her walk through the shop, risk her mingling with customers or bothering Gran.

All signs of the sultry smile were gone as she pressed her red lips together, but she moved toward the door. He opened it for her, and she leaned close to his ear. "You'll regret this, Mr. Ferryman. I offered to buy at market value. I would hate for that value to lessen."

"Leave. Now." Luke barely resisted slamming the door once she finally left.

He doubted the woman's threats were inconsequential, but what could she do to damage the bakery? If she wanted the building, she couldn't harm the structure. Perhaps she'd lure away customers?

Luke rubbed his neck. This day had gone from disgruntled to worse. His head ached.

"There you are." Gran bustled into the kitchen. "Stop your woolgathering and ... are you feeling alright?"

"I'm fine, Gran." He tried to smile. Gran planted fists on her hips, clearly suspicious.

"That woman caused this, didn't she?" Gran scowled at the side door. She must have realized Miss Walker had exited that way. "Go. Clear your head. I can manage things here."

"I won't leave you to manage the bakery alone. I'll be fine."

Gran glanced over her shoulder at the shop, then closed the door between the customers and the kitchen. "Luke, your grandfather is not getting younger. You will need to take over ferry duties soon. Without your help, I can manage an afternoon, but I will not be able to keep up the bakery."

It's what he knew, feared. "I don't want to sell."

"But if you don't marry, this offer may be our only other choice."

"Why does it have to be between those two choices? Why can't I hire a business manager? Someone who can help you when I have to operate the ferry."

Gran said nothing, not that there was anything to say. Luke knew what he suggested was impossible. They couldn't afford to hire someone. They barely scraped by as it was, especially the last few years.

Luke bowed his head. "I know you wish to see me favorably married. I want that, too. But I also want to marry for love. Like my parents, like you. Not simply to save the bakery."

Gran pulled him into a hug. She was a sturdy woman with plenty of padding, but beneath, he could feel her frail bones. She was aging. Slowing.

He pulled away. "Do you think Margherita is the answer?"

"Answer?" Gran chuckled. "When Reverend Charles asked whether we'd be willing to take in a refugee, Henry and I didn't hesitate. A young woman needed our help. We answered. But once she arrived ... well, I ..."

Luke cocked his head at the fondness he saw in his grandmother's expression. "She's likable, isn't she?" He could admit it.

Gran patted his arm. "I miss your sister. I miss having a granddaughter. And Margherita has the makings of one. I suppose I got ahead of myself, wishing you two together."

Somehow, it eased the angst he'd had earlier in the day, knowing his grandmother approved so highly of Margherita. It opened something in him he'd been barring against.

"I also don't like the idea of selling the bakery, especially to that Walker woman. However, the expectation for you to run the ferry is not negotiable. This town needs a ferry. But what you do with the bakery—sell or marry—I will leave that choice to you."

The counter bell dinged from the other room, and Luke and Gran shared a chagrined look. They'd been neglecting their customers while talking about the bakery's future.

"I'm not the ferryman yet." He draped his arm over Gran's shoulders and opened the door to the shop. "So today, let's be bakers together."

"You're a good man, Luke." She patted his chest, then added in a whisper, "I suspect she thinks so, too."

Luke laughed. Gran would always be a matchmaker, and he loved her for it.

As he stepped behind the counter, however, sadness pulled at the smile he offered his customer. The bakery was as much part of his heritage as the ferry. He hated the idea of losing it.

Was Margherita the answer? Was she someone he could grow to love?

Thought of her in his arms caused him to miscount the change his customer required.

Yeah, he supposed he might be half-way there already. Was she?

Chapter Eight

RAIN POURED OUTSIDE AS Margherita lifted the scone dough from the bowl and plopped it onto the floured surface of the table. Each day, she felt more confident that she had the right consistency for the Ferryman's signature scones. If only she wasn't so distracted by the pain in her leg today.

She adjusted her seat on the stool to have better leverage to knead the dough. Luca removed the first batch of rolls from the oven.

He had said hardly a word since they left the house. While not unusual, he also hadn't commented on her exaggerated limp. Not that she was looking for pity, of course. Only ... she missed his attentiveness. And she didn't know what to do with that feeling. It rubbed against the slim hold she had on the frustration caused by the pain. Made her uneasy.

The back door opened, and Margherita jumped. The quirk of Luca's brow said he noticed. So maybe he wasn't as inattentive as she thought. Then why so quiet?

Signora Ferryman, along with what seemed like a whole bucket of rain, blew in. "It is blustery out there, and the sea is in a tizzy. I could hardly walk here with that wind."

Luca helped his nonna with her coat. "Customers will appreciate their cuppa today."

Margherita kneaded the scone dough. Had she done something wrong? Some cultural thing she didn't understand? She'd heard all about the stoic British, but she'd experienced Luca's soft heart. Why did he treat her differently today?

"The extra customers will be a blessing." Signora Ferryman traded her damp hat for the mob cap she wore while baking. "Be sure to make extra pastries."

Pasticcino.

The Italian word for *pastries* floated through Margherita's mind, bringing with it warm memories of baking with Maria and Bella.

Margherita shaped the scone dough into circles. What if ... She glanced at Luca, then at his nonna. Her stomach knotted. No, she couldn't offer.

A wave of homesickness washed over her as the lighthouse light flashed into the bakery. "Might I make a *pasticcino italiano*?" The question slipped out, Italian and all.

Heat speared her. She brushed her warm cheek with her shoulder and pinned her gaze on the doughy rounds.

"What was that, dear?" Signora Ferryman wrapped her apron around her middle.

Now she'd really done it. Offering one of her recipes in their bakery. They'd kick her out for her impudence, for sure.

"Past-e-ch ..." Luca shook his head. "*Pasticcino.* Ha! I said it! What did I say?"

"Sounds like pastry." Signora Ferryman cocked her head, curiosity in her eyes.

Perhaps Margherita had not overstepped. They both seemed as if they genuinely desired to know more. Could they be sincerely interested in her recipe?

Luca crossed his arms, his muscles on full display. "I don't think she is going to tell us, Gran. Probably sore at me for being an absolute bore today."

Gran clucked her tongue. "You have been quiet—more quiet—since that Walker woman visited yesterday. You're not worried about her, are you?"

The Walker woman again? Margherita quartered the scone rounds. Hid a grimace as she caught her balance on one of the stool's rungs.

Luca appeared at her side with the oven paddle. Instead of scooping up the uncooked scones, he paused. "Should I take you home?"

Margherita's cheeks heated. He had noticed her pain. "When the rain lessens." She waved at the window as a gust of wind splattered droplets against it.

Luca studied her for a moment, then slid the paddle under the scone dough. "So this Italian pastry ... what did you have in mind?"

She glanced at Signora Ferryman, who nodded encouragement before she added a log to the oven. Margherita swallowed, smoothed the apron that lay over her thighs. Why was she so nervous about telling them? It was just a recipe.

"*Sfogliatella,*" she declared. It originated from her province of Campania. The flaky crust, the ricotta filling, the candied fruit—

"Fog ... fogli ..." Luca frowned. "Not going to get that one."

"It is not the easiest to say," Margherita chuckled, looking up at him, "but it is delicious."

Luca's gaze darted over her face. Did he lean closer? The handle of the oven paddle separated them, but his presence encircled her. Her eyes drifted closed as she remembered the comfort of being in his arms that first day, the way he caught her fall a week later. Never did she want to link her life with a man who might turn against her, as Paulo had done, but Luca wasn't Paulo. And how she craved a protector who—

"Luke." Signore Ferryman sliced into the moment and Margherita's eyes snapped open. "Begin another scone batch with different dried fruit than the one Margherita just finished."

Luca blinked, it taking him longer than her to emerge from whatever had wrapped around them. Was that frown one of regret? Margherita's heart *ker-thumped*.

Signora Ferryman huffed. "Luke, get those scones in the oven. Margherita, what are these Italian pastries made of? Do you think we have the ingredients?"

"Not all of them, I am sure." Margherita refocused, finding it easier when Luke moved away to slide the scones into the oven. "For one, the recipe calls for ricotta."

"And that is?" Signora Ferryman prompted as she brought over a bucket of berries.

"A *forma* ..." Why was English so difficult sometimes? She translated the Italian word in her head, triumphant when it took only a moment. "Cheese!"

"We can get that." Luca stayed on the opposite side of the table as he mixed the scone ingredients. "It won't be Italian milk, but still the same texture."

"It also uses semolina flour, but the other ingredients you use already." Margherita held up the orange she was about to slice through to make the scone glaze. "Like the peel of this little fruit."

"Wonderful!" Signora Ferryman wrapped the rolls in a cloth and placed them in the basket. "Luke, stop at the dairy after your deliveries this morning. I'm going to open the shop, and this afternoon we'll experiment."

After the older lady bustled away, Margherita slid from the stool, stuck her crutches under her arms, and went to the pantry to search for the ingredients. She felt Luca's eyes on her. Thankfully, he didn't offer to help her. She'd ask if she needed it, but too often people assumed she was incapable because of her leg. People like Paulo. *Inadatta.* Luca didn't make her feel unfit. He made her feel ... jittery, but in a warm, wonderful, anticipatory way.

The oven sputtered and crackled. She turned. "I have never heard it make that sound."

Luke leaned on his hands, which were nearly elbow deep in scone dough. "I must have filled the woodbox with a few overly wet logs. Can you grab ..." He frowned.

Her spine stiffened. Afraid of what he would say, she bit her lip. She could ease the awkward pause by saying something, but doubt reared its head again. What if he wasn't the man she thought he was? What if he acted like Paulo? *He's not Paulo.* Hadn't she just reached that conclusion?

Luke met her gaze. "Are you able to carry a log?" No condescension. Merely looking for information.

"I am." She hoped. His angular jaw bounced as if he were keeping back words. What words? Would his kindness evaporate eventually? With Paulo, she hadn't seen it until he nearly killed her.

He raised dough-covered fingers. "I would get a fresh log, but ... can you manage? Or call Gran? If my request causes you harm, say *no*. Please."

Her mouth dropped open. If she were a glaze, she'd melt right to the floor. Luca was not Paulo. Not even close. He wasn't thinking her incapable, he was worried about her. Strength filled her. "I can manage. I will go slow."

Luca nodded, but continued to watch her with concern. Attempting to ignore his attention—ironic considering she'd wondered why he hadn't been paying attention to her the entire morning—she stepped outside.

The rain had lessened only slightly, and it dampened her shoulders as she crossed the open space to the woodpile. The pile itself sat within an open outhouse that protected it from the worst of the inclement weather. She selected the two lightest logs she could find and tucked them between her torso and her crutches. Highly inefficient. And hard on her arm muscles.

Wisdom suggested she allow Luca or Signora Ferryman to do this job, but Margherita missed feeling valued. The taste she got as they asked about the pastry recipe had obviously gone to her head. Carrying these logs back to the bakery was nearly impossible. But she did it. And the proud look Luca gave her when she returned was worth the attempt.

She placed the logs in the oven, using tongs to set them in the hottest part of the ashes. Then she slid the baked scones onto the oven paddle and rescued them from the heat. Admiration shone in Luca's eyes and Margherita grinned. She was helping, proving her worth. She—

A *whoosh* exploded within the oven, then heat spewed out its mouth. Margherita screamed as fire seared her shoulder. She dropped to the floor. Scones rolled in all directions. And she was back in her home the night Paulo had tried to burn her alive.

Smoke billowed around her as she crawled from her bed. Fire climbed the walls with greedy hunger. Heat pressed in from all sides.

"Witch!" Paulo shouted over the fire's crackling. "You know you deserve to die."

Choking, coughing, crying ... she gathered her mandolin to her chest. Would he let her leave the house?

"Witch! Burn witch!" Shouts echoed Paulo's, swirling in her ears as embers danced in her room.

Then arms encircled her. She fought them, but the smell of citrus overcame the smoke and memories.

The next instant, Luca had carried her outside into the rain, an explosion of fire chasing them from the bakery.

Here she was in his arms again. Her skin burned. Her nerves jangled. Tears leaked down her cheeks. She turned her face into his shoulder, feeling oh-so weak. Gone was the strength, the desire for Luca's admiration. Perhaps he sensed her need because his hold tightened as they crossed the back garden. In fact, he must have because when he stepped beneath the woodpile's overhang, he rested his cheek against her hair, pressing her nose into his neck.

"I need to go back." His voice rumbled beneath her. Then he set her against the woodpile, probed her shoulder for a moment, pulling the charred fabric away from her damaged skin. She gasped at the pain of it, and he stopped.

Before she could say a word, he dashed a damp curl from her cheek, then demanded she stay put, and ran back toward the burning building.

She tucked her knees to her chest. Tears mingled with the rainwater dripping down her face from her hair. Her shoulder ached and without Luca's presence, the memories roared back. Last time she'd been caught in a fire, the smoke—not the flames—had almost killed her. She'd waited until she could hardly breathe before escaping into the night. Padre Benedict had hidden her, moved her from house to house while he worked to get her out of Italy.

Paulo had thought she died in the fire, a life-saving reprieve. Until he realized she survived. Then he turned the town against her. He labeled her a witch and Margherita knew she had to escape Italy, by whatever means necessary. Becoming smuggled cargo had saved her life. Because had the Ferrymans not welcomed her, she would not have survived much longer.

She blinked her vision clear. That was the past. It had been weeks. Surely she was free of Paulo now. Her shoulder twinged, her heart echoing the pain. Had her determination to prove her worth just destroyed the safety she felt here? The Ferryman family may have been willing to experiment with her Italian recipe, but they wouldn't want someone around who burned down their business. She was no better than that Walker woman, taking their bakery from them.

No, not taking. She hadn't done it on purpose, though she must have done something wrong. Had she selected the wrong type of logs? Were they too small? Had she placed them in the oven the wrong way? Had they been too wet?

She pressed the heels of her palms into her eye sockets, trying to walk through every moment leading up to the ball of fire that had exploded from the oven. She'd chosen the logs based on their size. If she couldn't lift them, carry them, she wouldn't have gotten them to the bakery. They were light, but were they too light? Had they been hollow, and that's why they exploded?

Could raindrops cause a fire? Her mamma—God rest her soul—would test the heat of a pan by sprinkling water into the oil. Had Margherita unwittingly done something similar? She couldn't remember. Nevertheless, she had not acted with malice. She'd wanted to help, not harm.

Would Luca know that? Believe that? Paulo wouldn't have.

Margherita dropped her forehead to her knees. Her leg aching, her arm aching, her whole body aching.

How much time had elapsed since Luca left her here? What were he and Signora Ferryman doing inside? Were they able to extinguish the fire?

Not only had she somehow caused their bakery to burn, she couldn't even help put out the fire.

Inutile.

A sob hiccupped through her, chased by a sense of panic. She couldn't even leave this spot. Her crutches had burned in the kitchen. She was trapped here until someone came to help. If they even remembered her here.

Incapace.

She wished she could dash away. Vanish into the rain. Not that her conscience would have allowed her to do so. She would have to wait. Wait for them to find her. Then face the Ferrymans, face Luca, like a woman of courage ought.

A gust dashed her with rain, and her tears fell. She wasn't brave. She wasn't strong. She was ... *senza valore.* Without value.

Words from Psalm 56 whispered across her soul in the voice of Padre Benedict. *Thou tellest my wanderings: put thou my tears into thy bottle: are they not in thy book?*

Il mio Dio ... her prayer vanished into the wind. Would He hear her? Would He answer? Was Padre Benedict—and the psalmist—right? Did God collect her every sorrow? Did He write each of them in His book? She was *niente,* nothing. Why would God deign to bend an ear to someone as ... broken ... as she?

Movement out of the corner of her eye caused her to glance up. Cautiously approaching was a sleek black cat. Margherita sniffed and held out her uninjured arm. The cat's whiskers twitched.

"Venire?" She wiggled her fingers, trying to coax the kitten closer. "Qui micio, micio."

The cat stepped toward her, and Margherita scratched it under the chin. A purring rumbled from the feline.

"You knew I needed a friend," she said to both the cat and God. For a few moments, the cat rubbed up against her, allowed her to pet it, then it bounded away.

"Margherita!" Luca called.

She raised her chin as he hurried out of the bakery toward her. Tears burned her eyes. The moment of reckoning tolled. Now she'd know the truth. Was Luca the noble man she thought him to be, or would he turn into Paulo and cast her upon the rubble heap?

Ah Signore Dio, aiuto.

Help.

Chapter Nine

L UCA HAD HATED TO leave Margherita behind, but what choice did he have? As soon as he had made sure Margherita was safe under the woodpile roof, he had torn himself away to check on Gran, the fire, and what state the bakery kitchen would be in after those flames had exploded from the oven.

Rain doused him as he jogged away from Margherita and turned his attention ahead. What would he find inside? It had taken but an instant for him to realize the danger as fire burst from the oven. Flour was flammable. Without a second hesitation, he had wrapped Margherita in his arms and charged outside. Flames had chased them. Even now, his back protested from the heat that had licked his shirt.

Luke glanced over his shoulder as he reached the bakery building. Margarita huddled against the woodpile, looking lost, alone, and scared. He swallowed. How could he leave her there without offering comfort? But he'd already given her an extra moment, could still feel her breath against his neck as he'd held her. Again.

He blustered out a breath, whispered a prayer, and turned the corner to the side door. Red blazed inside. The entire interior of the kitchen was burning. Nausea churned as he choked on the smoke. They'd lose the bakery. Gran's legacy—Gran!

Luke raced around to the front of the bakery and burst inside. Smoke billowed, causing his eyes to water. He covered his mouth with his apron. Where was Gran? Had she gotten out? He'd been so concerned with Margherita, he'd neglected his grandmother! What kind of grandson was he?

"Luke!" Gran waddled in behind him, a sloshing bucket of water in her hands.

Relief buckled his knees, and he caught himself against the hot wall.

"Stand up, young man." She shoved the bucket of water at him. "The Bucket Brigade is coming. Where is Margherita?"

Gran was safe. *Thank you, Lord.* "Margherita is by the woodpile. She's fine." It's what Gran wanted to hear, though he doubted the truth of that statement. Margherita was not fine. But he forced his roiling emotions behind a locked door as Gran expected.

He tossed the water into the fiery kitchen. Too little to make even a dent.

No more words were exchanged as neighbors rushed in to help them put out the fire. A line of them stretched out the door and bucket after bucket was passed to Luke. Determined to contain the fire to the kitchen, he tossed water into the flames. His muscles ached, his face burned, but he would not stop.

Slowly, ever so slowly, they got the upper hand on the fire as it ran out of fuel.

Once the flames died to smoldering flickers, Luca could take a moment to assess the damage. The kitchen was a burned-up hole, with a blackened clay ceiling and stained stone walls. The window glass had been blown to pieces. Anything that could burn—wooden spoons, flour sacks, even the stools—was gone.

Luke rested his hands atop his head. What had caused the fire? The last thing he remembered before heat burst from the oven was Margarita placing the smallest of logs into the fire. He hadn't wanted her to get the logs in the first place, but had seen she needed to help. The logs she'd brought in had actually made him smile. How proud he'd been of her, carrying them tucked between her body and the crutches. Resourceful. Creative. He'd almost kissed her, too. Earlier. Before Gran interrupted.

Oh Margherita. He needed to check on her. Would she still be out by the woodpile? He hoped somebody had seen her and helped. He already felt horrible for deserting her there. What she must think of him. Dumping her out back like a sack of flour.

Embarrassment worked into his cheeks. He'd go out there now and make sure someone had found her. Surely Gran had come to her aid by now.

"Know what caused this?" Constable Bailey tossed another bucket of water onto a smoldering bit of what used to be the table, stopping Luke from reaching the side door. The middle-aged man wore a bushy brown mustache. Long sideburns filled out his face. The man wore a wedding band, though Luke knew nothing about his wife. In fact, he knew little about the constable. Only that he was sent here in March for a short-term assignment.

Luke shook his head. "Nothing out of the ordinary, from what I could tell." He wouldn't mention Margherita. She had not done this on purpose. He knew that down to his marrow. However, a niggling sense of unease didn't allow him to brush off the fire as an accident, either. Alice Walker's supposed threat hovered too near. But what would she gain from burning them out of the bakery? She wanted to buy the building, after all.

"There is a rumor of a stranger living in town." Constable Bailey swung the empty bucket. "Know anything about that?"

Luke cast him a sideways glance. Obviously, he'd have to change tactics, but how much did the man know about Margherita? "There are always strangers in town. We get lots of tourists and visitors. The ferry brings in strangers every day. What is this rumor you heard?"

"A dark-haired woman with a limp has been seen walking with you for multiple days in a row. And not just walking with you, Mr. Ferryman, but joining you here in the bakery. Every morning. Find yourself a woman?"

Luke flinched. The gossips had been busy. Perhaps hiding Margherita hadn't been the wise choice after all.

"Surely she was here when the fire exploded." Bailey's questioning turned pointed. "Where might she have run off to?"

Did that mean no one had seen her out back? Gran must have found her, then.

"Relief, Mr. Ferryman?" Bailey raised his brows. "Why don't you want anyone to know about your relationship with this woman?"

How could he answer that? And where were Gran and Reverend Charles when he needed them? They were the ones who brought Margherita to Eden Cove, not Luke. Smuggling her into the country, hiding her in their home ... not Luke's idea. Protecting her, however, was another matter. Luke desired Gran's wisdom to know what to say, and the vicar's advice on how much to reveal of Margherita's presence here. Was it even safe to tell the constable the truth?

Not all of it. He would not tell Bailey how Margherita came to the country. That meant he would need to fabricate a story. Lie. Not just to save his own skin, since he was the one who actually brought her here illegally. More so, to tell

Bailey would be to admit to Margherita's illegal presence. He couldn't risk that. The constable would report her, deport her. And Margherita could not go back to Italy.

"Luke." The warning in Bailey's tone forced Luke to make a choice.

"She arrived here on the ferry a couple of weeks ago." The truth, if not the whole truth.

"And?" Bailey pressed.

"And nothing. Her father—" That's what they called the reverend in Italy, wasn't it? "—knows the vicar, who suggested she help Gran with the bakery. So she's been staying with us."

Bailey raised an eyebrow. "Attempting to make a match, are they?"

Luke reddened, though oddly, he didn't mind. It took the constable's attention from *how* Margherita got here to *why* she was here. He shrugged, needing to escape and end this questioning on a positive note so he could find Margherita. He headed for the side door. "I should check on Gran."

"Ah, but you didn't tell me the woman's name."

Luke froze.

"Nor where she was when the fire happened." He felt Bailey approach, but wouldn't look at him.

"She didn't do this," he ground out.

"You care about her." Bailey circled in front of him. "Are you covering for her?"

Was he? He raised his chin. "No."

"Blinded, then."

"No!"

Bailey raised both eyebrows. It irritated Luke, the constable's silent questioning. He wanted to demand the man spit out what he wanted to ask, but then Luke might have to utter a complete lie.

Luke blew out a breath. "Come with me."

He didn't give himself a chance to reconsider, but marched out the burned up side door. They couldn't hide Margherita any longer. The only hope, then, was for Bailey to see Margherita as a person who needed protecting. Then, perhaps, he wouldn't charge her with a crime she didn't commit or dig into her past. Much. She'd arrived with papers—likely forged. Would that be enough?

He rounded the corner of the bakery. Margherita still sat against the woodpile, her forehead on her knees. His step stuttered. No one had found her? The thought pierced, and her name burst from his lips. She looked up, and he broke into a jog. She had no crutches to help her walk, leaving her, essentially, trapped in the open structure. Without recourse, rain could have soaked her, chilled her.

What kind of man was he? Thinking to protect her and here he'd left her alone beside a *woodpile*! Like refuse. *Oh, Lord, forgive me!*

He should have sent someone to take her home. But they'd needed everyone to battle the fire. And it would have meant revealing her to the town. Excuses, all!

"That her?" Bailey kept pace.

Luke grunted, still unsure exactly what to say next. Rational thought disintegrated the closer they drew. Margherita's round face was sooty and tear-stained. Her black curls a mass around her head. The handkerchief she usually used to keep it contained was now wrapped around her injured shoulder. A physician would need to see to it. Another person to know of Margherita's presence. Their time of hiding her had ended.

"Luca?" Her quiet question punctured. She had placed her trust in him, and he'd brought a constable.

He dropped to his knees before her, searched her face for ... he didn't even know. "I'm sorry, Margherita. So sorry for leaving you here. Can you forgive me?"

Her brown eyes widened. "Forgive you?"

His pulse pounded. "I deserted you. I—"

"You had to." Her gaze darted to Bailey. "The bakery ... it burned for so long."

His chin dropped. He couldn't be selfish, begging her to absolve him. But how could he reassure her, protect her?

"I'm Constable Bailey." The man crouched beside him. Did he recognize Margherita's vulnerability? "I see you have an injury. You were in the bakery when the fire began?"

She washed pale, and she looked at Luke with eyes that begged for him to save her. He took her hand. "I told Constable Bailey your father sent you to stay with us, and you've been helping Gran in the bakery. Of course, Bailey needs to interview everyone who was in the kitchen when the fire started."

Her grip tightened around his fingers, tears shimmered in her eyes.

Luke clenched his jaw. He wouldn't put her through this. Not now, while soot still marred her skin. "Bailey, your questions have to wait. She's hurt. I need to take her home."

"There you are!" Gran bustled toward them. *Thank you, Lord*! Though why hadn't Gran found their guest before now? "Margherita, dear, are you all right?"

"She has a burn on her shoulder." Luke spoke before either Bailey or Margherita could derail Gran's rescue.

As he expected, his grandmother *tut-tut*-ed and took command of the situation. Bailey, she sent to secure her bakery, not brooking any argument the constable may have attempted. With the same insistence, she instructed Luke to carry Margherita home. Margherita protested, but Luke winked at her and she gave up. He wanted to take her home. Carry her home. Penance, perhaps. Or selfishness. At least she agreed.

Luke took a circuitous route toward the lighthouse to avoid the crowd gathered to help Gran with the bakery. No need to cause more gossip until they had a plan in place to manage it.

He walked slowly, his muscles tired from putting out the fire. Not that Margherita was heavy by any means.

"You can put me down." Margherita looked at him from under long black eyelashes. "Your gran cannot see us now."

He stopped near the lighthouse. The crash of the surf threatening to steal their words. "What if I don't want to put you down?" The question burned his neck and he couldn't look at her.

"Luca?"

He couldn't discern her tone, his heart pounded too hard in his ears. "I like this habit we've developed. Me saving a damsel in distress. Feeds my boyhood dreams of being a knight of the realm."

She laughed, and he tightened his hold. Had he ever heard her laugh in such a carefree way?

"I really am sorry for leaving you alone for so long." He had to say it again, even though it stole her smile.

"You are not mad at me?" It was more of a statement than a question and caused him to look at her. Her black brows were knit together, as if concentrating on unraveling a puzzle.

"Why would I be mad? I'm only grateful you weren't hurt worse. The explosion was not your fault. It was ... well, I don't know what it was, but it could have killed you."

She wiggled, forcing him to put her down or drop her. She gripped his arm to keep her balance and his focus on her. "You ... you did not want it to kill me."

He stumbled back a step, loosening her hold, and he jumped forward again before she could tumble. "Of course not. This Paulo really hurt you. Wanting you to die is not … it is not love, Margherita. It is hate."

"He hates me."

"And corrupted your neighbors to hate you." Like a cold North Sea wave, he realized the root of her doubt. "Margherita, that won't happen to me."

"How can you know that?" Desperation laced her question.

He caught her shoulders, bent to peer into her eyes as if he could deliver his words directly to her heart. "Because I love God. And if my heart is so full of love for Him, there is no room for hate. Loving my neighbor is merely an overflow."

A tremulous smile. "That is how I feel about music."

"Music?" Had he ever heard her sing?

"I play the mandolin."

"The third stick in your satchel the day you arrived."

Margherita nodded. "When I play, it is like *Dio,* He fills my heart and it flows out my fingers."

Luke couldn't find words to respond, so he stepped close and wrapped his arms around her, supporting her weight so her good leg wouldn't tire. She folded against him and he rested his cheek against her hair. She smelled of smoke, of wood, and he held her more tightly. God had spared her life today. Bringing her here had saved her life, as well.

"I am a privileged man, Margherita." What had Reverend Charles said? To welcome the stranger and in doing so, you welcome God? "You are a special woman. I am humbled that God would allow me a role in saving you."

Margherita patted his chest, then pushed away. "It seems hiding here is done."

"You can't mean to leave." The words escaped before he could think better of them.

"No." She smiled. "I have an idea of how to save the bakery. I will play my mandolin for your neighbors as a thank-you for helping rebuild."

"But then you'll be out in the open." The absence of fear in her eyes cast away his doubts. "Are you sure?"

"I have prayed for a way to show my thankfulness." Her shoulders squared, even as she still leaned on him for support. "It is time."

"Then I shall get you a new set of crutches, m'lady." He cupped her cheek. "And perhaps steal a kiss?"

Heat warmed his palm, and she lowered her lashes. "*Sì*, Luca. You may."

Chapter Ten

MARGHERITA BRACED FOR LUCA'S kiss. One part anticipation, one part fear. Paulo had been the only man who'd ever kissed her. She never thought she'd want another from any man, but after hearing Luca's declaration of his love for God ... she felt as if an invisible string had tied her to Luca. Tugging her closer.

Or was that his arm around her waist?

He held her carefully, leaving no risk of her losing her balance or fatiguing her good leg. Ever since the day he helped her down the rope ladder out on the river, he had cared for her in such a way. Supporting, not demeaning. It gave her strength. So unlike Paulo, it embarrassed her that she could worry the two men were similar.

Mamma Mia! Had time stood still? She kept her eyes closed, suddenly afraid of what she'd see. Her pulse competed with the crash of waves behind her. Was Luca second guessing his request? Did he mean he'd steal a kiss another time? Perhaps she had made a fool of herself. Been swept away by—

His lips touched hers. Gentle. Light. Then gone.

She sagged against the arm that held her. She hadn't been mistaken. He'd kissed her. And not at all like Paulo, who had always driven a kiss with—Luca's lips found hers again and thoughts of her former fiancé vanished.

Emotion welled as she sank beneath Luca's kiss. How, when it was gentle, caressing. Sunlight, not storm. Ah! She could weep at the tenderness of it.

"You're crying." His voice was rough as he ran his thumb over her cheek. Was she?

"Another?" Oh, she was pitiful, and the tears threatened to turn into a sob. But something in Luca's touch healed her.

He obliged her, a smile curving his lips until he broke away with a shake of his head. "I can't stop grinning."

And she couldn't stop the tears. Or her smile. She ducked her head even as hope bloomed deep within her soul. Like a musical score that began pianissimo and crescendoed as the full orchestra joined in.

"I admit to being confused." Luca tapped her chin to bring her gaze to his. Blue lake eyes, both sparkling in the sunlight and darkened with concern. "Are you alright?"

"*Si, si, molto bene.*" Yet more tears flowed. She pressed up onto the toes of her good foot to give him a quick kiss. Bold, yes, but she wished to reassure him. "I am good, Luca. I am free."

"Free?" He rested his forehead on hers. "I am glad, Margherita. So glad."

They stood like that, together, until her tears finally stopped. Then Margherita leaned on Luca's arm as they slowly made their way back to 1 Sycamore. Such joy filled her heart that she babbled the entire way about her idea to perform for the people of Eden Cove. She hadn't played for people since before the earthquake, but she used to love it. Music was a gift God had given her and the opportunity to share it, use it, brought a peace she hadn't felt since the building had collapsed around her and Maria.

How had a kiss unlocked this part of her that had been buried since then? Luca's kiss. It was more than the physical act of his lips on hers—a delightful sensation, of course—it was his words before he kissed her. The kiss felt more like a seal. A promise. And it opened her heart to receive his assurances.

How did she ever think Luca would succumb to hate? The burning of the bakery offered the perfect opportunity. Paulo would have ... would have left her in the building and then blamed her for all the world to hear. The constable would have arrested her. The town, who hadn't even known of her existence, would have vilified her.

Instead, Luca had begged for forgiveness. Had defended her to the constable. Had refused to lay blame on her shoulders. The truth of that washed over her like the waves of the North Sea beside them.

Tears smarted her eyes, and she leaned on Luca's arm even more.

"Is it your leg?" Luca stopped them near the sycamore tree his great-grandfather planted. "Should I carry you?"

She couldn't help smiling. "You just want to carry me."

"Perhaps." He frowned. "But you are crying again. Why?"

She brushed her cheeks. "I am thanking God for you, Luca."

Instead of her words lightening his worry, a pensive expression stole over his face.

"What is it, Luca? Tell me."

"This tree is special in my family, though Grandad refuses to talk about why." Luca knelt and brushed dirt from a small stone plaque. He traced the initials LF that had been carved into the stone alongside a date from 1853. Ten years before Signore was born, according to the family tree she'd found.

She wanted to ask, but sensed if she spoke, Luca would change the subject, and she wanted to hear his thoughts. A minute passed, and a duck landed in the pond beyond. Then finally Luca spoke.

"Even if we rebuild the bakery kitchen, I won't be able to run it. I'm a Ferryman, and so the next ferryman." His mouth tipped up in a type of smile as he rose. "The bakery is Gran's legacy. The ferry is Grandad's. I am one person. How can I choose which legacy to continue? Eden Cove needs both. What should I do, Margherita?"

The way he asked, the way his gaze stayed pinned on the plaque at the base of the old sycamore ... he was reaching out for help. Her help.

"What does your spirit tell you?" she asked. "You love God. His Spirito Santo—how do you say it in English?"

"Spirit? Holy Spirit?"

Margherita nodded. "Si, si. His Holy Spirit whispers the answer to you. Have you asked God?"

"Reverend Charles suggested I ask you about your view of God." He shook his head. "I need to get back to the bakery, but my feet won't take me."

"You are torn, Luca." Margherita rested her head against his arm, which she still held to keep her balance. "As I sat beside the woodpile, I asked whether God could see me. Whether He gathered my tears. And then you spoke of God's love and how it drives out hate. God heard me, Luca. He will hear you, too."

Luca's lashes fluttered. Was he attempting not to cry? She gripped his arm tighter. His throat bobbed. Then he glanced down at her. "Would you join me at my church?"

He wanted her to attend church with him? She nodded, longing to visit the Lord's house again.

"Come on." He turned them toward 1 Sycamore. "Let's get you ..."

"Home?"

He covered her hands with his free one. And Margherita stayed quiet, letting his words tumble around in her mind. She stretched them like her nonna did to dough when she made pasta. Rolling them. Cutting them. Letting them dry. All while Luca settled her in the family parlor with a cup of tea and a biscuit, her bad leg propped up with pillows.

He promised to send the doctor to check on her as soon as possible—the ache in her shoulder had blended with the pain in her leg so that she almost forgot about it—and would find her crutches by the end of the day. The house quieted. It would be hours before the housekeeper returned to make the evening meal. And the bakery disaster would keep the Ferrymans busy for quite some time, she knew.

Margherita rested her head against the cushion. Why had Luca asked her about attending services with him? She knew Eden Cove did not have a Catholic Church, so Luca's would be part of the Church of England, most likely. She missed services. Missed Padre Benedict's blessings. Was the older man all right? Had Paulo harmed him because of her? Reverend Car ... Charles—his name was getting easier to say—had not heard from his friend.

Now that there was no need to hide, she would attend services with Luca and his family. It would be odd going to a service that was not what she was accustomed to, and some wouldn't understand, but Padre Benedict respected Reverend

Charles. Trusted him with her life, considering how he'd sent her here. She could trust him with her spiritual life, too.

At the arrival of Signora Ferryman with the doctor, all other thoughts vanished from Margherita's mind. He assessed her leg, brought her crutches, and treated her shoulder. Cleaning the burn took the last of her strength. She lived with pain. Had learned to manage a lot. However, whatever the doctor had to do to her shoulder shoved her past the precipice. She was glad Luca wasn't here to see her tears, to hear her cries. Signora Ferryman held her, and she clung to the older woman.

Finally, the pain medicine the doctor administered took effect and Margherita drifted into oblivion. At some point, voices broke through the fog, arms lifted her, and a blanket covered her. She relaxed into the pillow beneath her head, slipping back into a drugged sleep until a female voice pulled her from the emptiness.

"Still sleeping," the voice huffed. "The morning is wasting away. What were they thinking, bringing this girl here?"

Margherita kept her eyes closed, her sluggish mind sifting through the English words, finally recognizing the speaker. Signora Archer, the housekeeper, must be here for her morning work. Margherita had slept the night through. Her stomach grumbled at having missed a meal or two.

"Worthless, worthless girl," Signora Archer muttered to herself. "Causing a fire, then not aiding the clean up. Probably trying to trap Luke into marrying her, too."

Margherita barely held in a gasp as the words struck the most tender place in her heart.

"Foreigners. They will be our ruin." Her bedroom door closed, shutting out the woman's words.

Margherita opened her eyes to stare at the ceiling. Pain flooded her from inside and out. Signora Archer didn't know Margherita, nor why the Ferrymans welcomed her. She didn't know the truth behind the fire, nor how Luca felt about it all. Then again, that was—apparently—yesterday. Had a new day changed anything? No. Luca said his actions toward her flowed from God's love, and even if Luca someday shut off that valve, God's love did not change. She must cling to that truth.

Nevertheless.

Ignorance and prejudice and hate had driven Margherita from her home, from her country. What if—despite all Luca said—it sent her fleeing Eden Cove, too? Luca was one person in a sea of people. What difference could he make?

Not wanting to stay in the house alone with Signora Archer, Margherita changed clothes, and tried out her new crutches. They didn't fit as well as her old ones, but they helped her walk, so they would do. She donned a coat as she waited until she heard Signora Archer leave the kitchen, then she slipped out the back door to visit the bagno.

Based on the sun's position, it was mid-morning. The air was fresh after yesterday's rain. Mild, too. Not as warm as home, of course, but not damp and chilly either. Would she grow accustomed to the difference in the weather? Would she be able to stay in Eden Cove long enough to find out?

Margherita made her way down the walk. She'd go to the bakery, see if she could help, and ask where she might find a bite of food. But her leg tired well before she reached the road that would take her across Eden Cove. She trudged on, forward her only option because going back meant facing Signora Archer.

Incapace.

The word whispered in her ear. Insidious. Hateful.

"Margherita." Signore Ferryman called from her left. She turned to see him waving her toward him. "I'm taking the ferry out. Join me."

She readily agreed and was soon settled in the very boat that had brought her to these shores.

"I make regular trips across the river, not knowing whether someone is waiting on the other side." The older man pulled at the oars. "Closing the ferry to help clear the rubbish from the bakery is not an option."

"You do not have to explain to me." Margherita fidgeted with the edge of the bandage covering her burn. It ached like her heart. "My leg will not let me help either."

Signore Ferryman studied her for a good minute, maybe two. She tried not to squirm under his assessment. Finally, he asked, "Would you like to try rowing?"

Che? "What? Me?"

"The muscle you have built using the crutches will benefit you. And your good leg is used to being your primary source of balance. Sit here."

He helped her switch places with him. An awkward dance, seeing that the boat rocked, throwing her off balance. They were laughing by the time she sat in the bow, her back facing the direction they headed.

Signore Ferryman showed her where to plant her good foot, then how to pull the oars. The boat glided through the water. She lifted the oars as he directed, then turned them parallel to the water before dropping them in to propel the boat forward again.

"You're a natural." He grinned at her, his round face lighting up.

For the first time since the rocks crushed her leg, she felt … capable. Baking she enjoyed, but this was incredible! She grinned back at Signore Ferryman. "I'm rowing a boat!"

Pride danced in his eyes. This man was proud of her?

"Grazie, Signore Ferryman." She pulled at the oars again, unable to stop smiling.

The burn on her shoulder didn't like the motion, but the rest of her muscles warmed with it. She kept her bad leg tucked beneath the bench seat, using the other to provide leverage. Across the river they went, smoothly cutting through the waves.

When they reached shore, Signore Ferryman had her stay seated while he helped a couple aboard. Tourists from London vacationing nearby. The four of them chatted amicably as Margherita rowed them back across the river. Never once did they seem to wonder why a woman was rowing instead of Signore Ferryman. When they reached the Eden Cove dock, they thanked her and went on their way.

Signore Ferryman crouched on the wooden dock, looking down at her. "Luke sees the ferry as his duty. He does not have the look in his eyes as you do right now."

"I have been useless for so long." The honest explanation slipped out.

He held up a meaty finger. "You are not useless. You have felt useless."

Margherita cocked her head.

"The difference is in how you see yourself. You've allowed others to view you in such a way. It is not the truth. You are useful, Margherita. God has a purpose for you."

"Do you know what that could be?" Even as she spoke the question, her words to Luca returned to her. Ask God, listen to the Spirito Santo.

Signore Ferryman waved at her leg. "Let me teach you how to get out of the boat." He had her toss her crutches to the dock, then step first with her bad leg. Because of the height difference from the boat to the dock, she put weight on the knee of her bad leg, not her injured foot. Once on all fours, Margherita could use her crutches to rise on her one good leg and find her balance.

"Not the most ladylike or dignified way of disembarking," Signore Ferryman crossed his arms, his eyes teasing, "but ya did it all on yer own."

Margherita glanced back at the boat, then at the old ferryman. "I sure did."

Friday, 25 September, 1931
Bella Matrone
Crow's Nest, Wisconsin
United States of America

Dearest Bella,

He kissed me.

I can hear you squeal from across the ocean! Settle down, now, so I might talk.

It began as a wonderful morning, helping Luca in the bakery. I even offered to share a recipe from home. Hush. I'm getting to the kiss. But much happened before then that I must tell you.

Ah Bella, the oven exploded!

I fear it was my fault, or at the very least, my pride, though I do not know what I did or how it happened. But it burned the inside of the bakery. Somehow, the building still stands, but I fear it must be gutted.

When Luca brought the constable to find me, I thought he would turn me in. I feared I would be sent back to Italia. But, Bella, he protected me from the constable's questions. He insisted they could wait and that I must be taken home.

And he carried me. Ah! Bella, I felt so safe in his arms. How can that be? You see, I lost my crutches in the fire and then we stopped by the edge of the North Sea. The bit before that is fuzzy because of his kiss. It healed something in my heart. I know it did.

Do not protest, il mia amica. He did not take advantage. Yes, I was distraught. The fire brought back horrible memories of what Paulo did to me. But, Bella, Luca is not Paulo. I see that now. He is good and kind and … and … no. I am not ready to say more. It is too dear and I must hold it close to my heart. You understand, don't you?

Pray for me, dearest Bella.

I am to meet the vicar in a few moments. He is helping me prepare for the mandolin concert I will perform to raise funds for the rebuilding of the bakery. We have been talking about God, faith, and church, too. He knows Padre Benedict. I have much to consider.

You will write soon?

Margherita

Chapter Eleven

LUKE DROPPED ONTO ONE of the new stools in the bakery kitchen. His every waking hour of the last week or so had been spent here, scrubbing the stone, airing out the shop front, hauling fresh supplies Gran purchased with a loan. Tomorrow they would reopen. Tomorrow Margherita would rejoin him here.

He scrubbed a hand over his mouth, remembering their kiss. He hadn't kissed her since. Not that he didn't wish to—he did, to distraction sometimes—but first he'd needed to rebuild the bakery. Focus on his family and their legacy.

Tonight, however, was Margherita's concert.

Reverend Charles was in charge of the event, which would take place in the grassy area by the waterfall. Afterward, the vicar would request donations for the bakery.

Luke closed his eyes, the prayer he'd prayed dozens of times this last week fresh in his heart. Would the Lord provide enough to pay back the loan tonight? Only the Ferryman reputation had allowed the bank to grant their request. If they had to sell the bakery because Luke could not run both the bakery and the ferry, they would still have to pay the loan. And he didn't know how he would support his grandparents on the ferry fare alone. Let alone hold hope to one day have a family of his own.

Which brought him back to Margherita. Their kiss. Her willingness to help his family, even if it put her at risk. He must have asked her a dozen times this past week whether she was sure about going through with the concert. Not once did she hesitate.

"What are you still doing here?" Gran bustled into the kitchen while removing her apron. "We must hurry home to freshen up or we'll be late."

He knew that, yet something held him here.

Gran planted fists on her hips. "What's got you tangled up?"

How to put into words this nebulous unease? Constable Bailey had accepted his and Gran's word that Margherita had no part in harming the bakery; however, his investigation had ended there. With no proof of foul play, sabotage, or any other suspect to question, what else could the constable do? Yet Alice Walker had not reappeared since. Why? It worried him.

"Are you planning to escort Margherita?" Gran urged him to his feet. "She'll leave for the waterfall without you. Go on. I'll lock up."

His nerves jittered. He and Margherita had not been alone since their kiss. Apparently, she had spent her time with Grandad on the ferry while Luke and Gran repaired the bakery. Not that Luke resented her absence. He had insisted she stay away so she wouldn't get hurt. Surprisingly, she had accepted his suggestion without protest and he had regretted his offer since. He missed her. Terribly.

Gran shooed him out the side door and he turned his feet toward 1 Sycamore, where Margherita readied for the evening. His pace quickened. Why had he stalled at the bakery? Minutes he could have spent with Margherita.

As he stepped through the front door and down the hall, he heard her crutches tapping the floor in her room. It spurred him into action. He took extra care to be freshly washed, impeccably dressed, and ready to escort the most beautiful woman in Eden Cove to her concert.

In no time at all, Luke leaned against the wall outside her room, waiting for her to open her door, nerves ratcheting up again. He'd have a moment alone with her. He'd have her on his arm. She would perform in front of the entire town. Would his neighbors welcome her?

"Luca," her lilting voice pulled him from his mental questions. She stood framed in her doorway, the satchel holding her mandolin hanging from her uninjured shoulder, her crutches tucked under her arms. She wore a flowing blue dress with little sleeves that covered her shoulders—but not the bandage that covered her burn. The fabric swished around her feet as she stepped toward him.

"You're gorgeous," the compliment slipped out in a whisper.

Her cheeks darkened, and she ducked her head. "Grazie."

He knew now that *grazie* meant thank you, and it made him ask, "How do you say 'very beautiful' in Italian? About a woman, not a house."

Her skin darkened even more, but her eyes twinkled. "*Molto bella.*"

"Molto bella." He imitated the way she rolled her Ls, and she flushed still more. It gave him a heady feeling, this ability to cause such a reaction in her. He grinned. "May I escort you tonight, m'lady?"

She nodded, her entire face a smile. *Molto bella* indeed.

As they walked toward the waterfall, which flowed out of the river that led from the Deben to Great Lake, across the water from the church, Margherita kept up a steady stream of chatter. He could listen to her talk all day. Her accent soothed. What she spoke about was interesting, too, but today he kept having to remind himself to tune in. He was distracted simply by being near her again.

"You have not heard a word I said." At least she laughed.

Luke shook his head. "How do you say 'sorry'?"

"*Mi dispiace.* What has you so distracted?"

His turn to redden. "I'm happy to see you."

She paused at the fork that led across the bridge to Castle on the Hill and St. Bart's. "Luca, I have a question."

"Anything."

She didn't smile as he hoped. Instead, she looked down at the cobbles beneath their feet.

"Margherita?" He cupped her cheek and she let him lift her chin. "What is it? You can tell me anything. Ask me anything. You know that, right?" Goodness, he might as well hand his heart to her on a platter right here and now.

She pressed her head into his touch. "What if …"

"What if?" He prompted, wanting to hear the rest of her wishful question.

"What if you did not become the ferryman?"

He gaped at her. Where had this question come from? "Why wouldn't I? It is my birthright. The expectation of my family. I am a Ferryman."

She adjusted her crutches, bringing her closer to him, and rested a palm against his chest. "I ask because you love the bakery."

Whether because of the heat of her touch or the truth of her words, something quaked inside him.

"Luca, this week has shown that most of all. Your passion and joy to rebuild it. You have poured your soul into it."

He couldn't deny it. "But someone has to run the ferry."

"Si, si."

"Then why offer a way out?" Had he really just asked that? "I didn't mean it that way."

She patted his chest, stopping words. "You did, Luca. I know it is how you feel. You may not admit to yourself or your nonni—grandparents—but I see."

What could he say? "I don't have a choice, Margherita."

"What if ..." She glanced toward the dock where Grandad should arrive shortly, after what would usually be his last run of the day. But tonight he'd offer to return any concert-goers across the river after it ended. Someday that would be him. "Luca, what if I did?"

"Did what? Run the ferry?" He stared at her. So small and feminine, balancing on her crutches, appearing so vulnerable beside him.

Then he blinked.

She turned her gaze on him, and he took a step back. Yes, she still ignited his sense of protection, but as the sun broke through the clouds, he saw her in a different light.

Before him stood the North Sea. Dark and full of deep emotion, able to sink a boat or carry it to new shores. Sunlight caused its spray to glitter like thousands of diamonds even as the waves crashed against towering rocks. Margherita was as strong as the sea. And as gentle as water. She belonged on the water. A pearl of great price, created through trial and hardship.

He cupped her cheek. "You would make a wonderful ferryman."

She offered a tiny pout. "*Traghettatrice*, you mean."

He laughed. "I'm not even going to try saying that."

"It means a female ferryman." She gave an impish smile. "I am also a *musicista*. And if I am to play a concert tonight, I cannot be late."

So much for the kiss he wanted to give her. Later. Tonight. Perhaps for a lifetime. Had he found the woman he would love for the rest of his life?

"But Luca? Think about it, si?"

There was no doubt that he would. The question stayed with him as he helped Margherita set up for her concert. The buzz of his neighbors swarmed around them. They had met Margherita at services this past Sunday. They seemed curious more than standoffish. Luke's own curiosity had been growing, too. He had yet to hear Margherita play her mandolin. In fact, he wasn't sure he had ever heard a mandolin.

Slowly, the grassy area filled with people. Some brought blankets as if for a picnic. A few others brought their dining chairs. He should have thought to do that for Gran and Grandad. He needn't have worried. Grandad brought a chair for each, leaving Luke to sit on the damp grass beside them. Mrs. Archer would have a fit at the mud, Luke was sure, but at the moment he didn't care. He was in the front row and the concert was about to begin.

The sun sat low in the sky as Reverend Charles encouraged the crowd to silence themselves. A cool breeze fluttered Margherita's skirt as she sat on a stool Reverend Charles had bought from the church. Her good leg hooked on a rung, her bad leg swung with a rhythm all her own. The kerchief around her hair held it away from her face, which she kept down-turned. Atop her knee rested the mandolin.

It looked like an oddly shaped violin, but held sideways across her lap. Under her right arm was the bowl of the instrument. It looked as big as she! How she wrapped her arm around it, Luke didn't know. But her fingers lightly plucked at the strings that ran across the hollow circle and up the neck. She turned the black pegs with her left, changing the pitch of the notes she played.

And then she smiled.

Luke's heart skittered as she caught his eye and straightened her shoulders. She was ready to play. She nodded to Reverend Charles.

"Dearly beloved," Reverend Charles's voice easily carried over the sound of the waterfall well behind the makeshift stage, "thank you for joining us today as we celebrate the re-opening of Ferryman's Bakery."

Applause pattered through the crowd.

"Margherita wished to bless the family who has hosted her these last few weeks. As I understand it, the instrument she will play—a mandolin—is a family heirloom passed down to her from her family, which originated in Italy."

Luke discovered a newfound respect for the old vicar, which seemed impossible considering in what high esteem he already held the man. But the way he described Margherita's past while glossing over the fact she'd been smuggled into the country mere weeks ago was brilliantly done.

"Afterwards, it is Margherita's and my wish that, if you enjoyed her concert, you would donate toward the rebuilding expenses one of our most esteemed families has incurred. Now, please join me in welcoming Margherita."

Luke clapped, but noted the vicar had not used Margherita's last name. Hiding her in plain sight. Would it be enough? Surely, after all this time, her former fiancé had tired of looking for her. How could his hate run so deep that he'd chase her to England? He shivered at the thought.

Margherita closed her eyes. A beautiful melody flowed from the mandolin, teased out by her dancing fingers. And then she sang.

> All creatures of our God and King
> Lift up your voice and with us sing,
> Alleluia! Alleluia!

Emotion pricked Luke's eyes. Though her accent curled around the words, she sang in English.

> Thou burning sun with golden beam,
> Thou silver moon with softer gleam!
> O praise Him! O praise Him!
> Alleluia! Alleluia! Alleluia!

What a gift she gave, learning a song they'd sung frequently at St. Bart's since sometime around the Great War. He knew it was even translated by a Church of England rector, a vicar named William H. Draper. This Catholic Italian had sung that song for them.

Verse after verse churned the emotion in his soul into a frothing sea. He did not deserve a woman like her. She would sacrifice everything, her home, her religion, her name, to marry him. How could he ask it of her?

And yet, the thought of not spending the rest of his life with her was an unbearable concept. He wanted to come home—from the bakery?—to hear her sing. Another sacrifice. She would willingly take on the ferryman position so he could bake. The bakery passed from mother to daughter, not grandmother to grand*son*. What was he thinking?

Margherita transitioned to another song, but the words were lost on Luke. His thoughts tumbled like the waterfall behind her. The melody dragged him into the undertow. He rested his elbows on his knees, hands clasped. Listening. Praying.

As the song switched again to something dramatic and stormy, Luke was reminded of the image of Margherita's likeness to the North Sea. She wasn't taking the job of ferryman just for him. The way her eyes gleamed as she pronounced that Italian word he couldn't even muddle through in his head told him that much. A female ferryman.

He tipped his head to watch her. She flowed with the music, her fingers moving faster than anything he'd seen before. Yet serenity glowed from her soul. God had created her with this love of music. How easy it was to fixate on how to help her, whether because of her leg or her refugee plight. She was more than either of those, and yet those hardships were such a part of her, they shaped this moment.

How he wanted to spare her, and that told him how much he'd come to care for her. She must have felt him watching her because she glanced up. Her gaze tangled with his. Was this love he felt for her? Aye, he would sacrifice for her. But he also must let her fly.

Margherita brought her music to a close with a dip of her chin and a smile. Gran sniffed beside Luke, surreptitiously dabbing her eyes. Around him, cheers and clapping grew, and then they were all standing. Her music had spoken to each of them.

Emotion clogged his throat again. How proud he was of her. He could not allow his desire to be her protector clip her wings.

A gleam lit Margherita's eye. "*Grazie*. Thank you. I shall leave you with a song from my family's homeland. It is called 'Tarantella Di Napoli.' Clap your hands with me."

Like the spark of a match, her fingers were off and the music skipped from her mandolin. Gran's toe tapped, then Grandad slapped his knee in time with the beat. Luke grinned and began to clap. Slowly, the music pulled this crowd of Englishmen from their even-keeled appreciation to joyous participation.

This was Margherita.

A last strum and the crowd broke into applause. Margherita beamed.

"Strega!" A voice boomed.

Everyone turned toward the blonde man who approached via the path, his face contorted in rage. One look at Margherita's ashen face and Luke knew. Her former fiancé had found her, and there was murder in his eyes.

Chapter Twelve

THE JOY OF THE last hour disintegrated to ash. Bile burned up Margherita's throat. She hadn't been this close to Paulo since before he tried to burn her house down around her. Her body trembled. If possible, the hate in his eyes burned even hotter than she'd ever seen.

How had he found her?

Chatter rolled through the crowd. Of course this confrontation would be public. No choice but to accept her fate. No more running, no more hiding. The last weeks had strengthened her, she would face Paulo. If the people of Eden Cove sent her away with him, then she would go.

Even if it meant her death.

Poor Luca. Signore and Signora Ferryman. And Reverend Charles, too.

Paulo stalked toward her, as if oblivious to the many eyes watching his every move. Time slowed. She slipped from the stool, laying her mandolin aside. Would the population of Eden Cove side with him, or her? The charismatic leader, broad shoulders, large muscles, the bearing of authority. Or the dark-haired stranger, the cripple, the useless one?

And then Luca stood between her and Paulo.

Margherita swayed and pressed a hand atop her stool to keep her balance. Paulo stopped his advance and like two Aryan gods, he and Luca faced one another. Of equal height and strength, yet one with hatred pouring from his expression, the other, protective anger.

"You are not welcome here," Luca declared. He knew Paulo's identity. Knew his purpose. Margherita wrapped her fingers over the edge of the stool as fear seized her muscles.

"Out of my way, Englishman." Paulo spat.

"No." Luca crossed his arms, showing his muscles.

The crowd murmured, but no one moved to leave—or intervene. Did they think this was a show? An act? Surely someone would stop these two men from locking horns. If only her own voice wasn't trapped in her throat or her leg too weak to walk. Luca could not be hurt because of her.

"I know why you've come here." Luca spoke firmly, calmly.

"To take back my *donna*." Paulo growled. Margherita squeezed her eyes shut against the word he'd used. She was not his woman. Not his lady. She wasn't his at all. Not any more.

"Donna?" Luca gave an amused chuckle. "No women here named Donna."

Oh Luca. She barely managed to shift out of the way as Paulo lunged at Luca. Luca dodged Paulo's fist. The crowd gasped. Shouts, whistles, cries all blended together as Margherita used the stool as a cane to try to stay out of the men's way. Her mangled leg cramped and tears pricked her eyes.

Even through her watery vision, she could see how Luca kept his back to her, kept himself between her and Paulo. *Oh Luca.*

"Stop it!" Reverend Charles stepped between the men, taking a fist to the chin for his efforts. "Stop right now!"

Paulo retreated, chest heaving. He sneered at Margherita and she shivered.

Luca again put himself between them. His hand covered hers where it rested on the stool. His shaking hand.

"Luca, *per favore* ..." She couldn't switch to English, so she pressed her lips together. His fingers wrapped around hers and squeezed.

"We are civilized gentlemen," Reverend Charles was saying. "We can have a civil conversation. Is that understood?"

"Absolutely," Luca declared, but Paulo said nothing.

She curled her fingers to hold on to Luca's, and the trembling eased. Before today, only Padre Benedict had stood between her and hate, now Luca did, too.

Not just Luca.

Signora Ferryman wrapped her arm around Margherita's shoulders, tugging Margherita away from Luca and the stool like a mother hen would her chick. Signore Ferryman flanked Luca as the vicar stepped from between Luca and Paulo. Did the crowd hold their collective breath as Margherita did? Waiting to see what Paulo would do next? The tinder would take but a spark to explode again.

And then realization struck Margherita, and she covered her mouth. The Ferrymans—Signore and Signora, and Luca—were one of the most established families of Eden Cove. They and the vicar declared before the entire town that they chose her. Supported her. She was one of their own now, and as such, would be protected.

Paulo must have realized the swing in her favor as well, because he stepped back. Not a retreat exactly, more of a reorganizing of his forces. Luca, once again her barrier from her former fiancé, spread his feet and crossed his arms. Signore Ferryman mirrored his stance. Two men used to balancing in a bobbing boat stood firm before the storm that was Paulo.

"How well do you know Margherita?" Though Paulo spoke calmly, his voice—devoid of an accent—carried across the crowd. A strike against flint.

"You need to leave." Luca advanced until the vicar caught his shoulder. "You need to leave. Now. This is not the time for this conversation."

Paulo held up his hand. "I think your neighbors deserve to know the witch they harbor."

Murmurs cascaded through the crowd.

"She is not a witch." Anger threaded Luca's words. "She is a woman forced to flee from the despicable hatred of the man who wanted to marry her."

Paulo's eyes widened, and the crowd's murmurs grew. Signora Ferryman wrapped Margherita in her arms, the protection of a mother, and Margherita clung to her.

"Yes." Luca continued. "I know her story. I know what happened and how she came to England. Because I brought her to Eden Cove."

Oh Luca. What are you saying?

"That is quite enough," Reverend Charles scolded. "We do not make a scene and we certainly do not air a person's story before the entire town."

Paulo smirked. They had no such qualms about that back home.

"I disagree, Reverend." Luca's declaration brought audible gasps this time. Even Signora Ferryman muttered under her breath.

"Son, are you sure?" Signore Ferryman spoke in an undertone.

"This is not a tableau the town needs to see," Signora Ferryman added.

"I am." Luca had not taken his focus from Paulo. "This man destroyed Margherita's reputation and I won't have him do that again. Enough hiding. The insidious hatred of turning people against one another ends now. Here. Today. And it begins by shining a beacon on the truth."

Paulo's grin widened. "I'll happily share all Margherita's wickedness. The way she broke my heart. Flaunted her supposed injury with those crutches."

"Enough!" Luca slashed his hand through the air, causing Signora Ferryman to jump. "I said we shall share the truth. Her injury is not feigned. I will not allow you to malign her."

"Gentlemen." Constable Bailey approached, taking a neutral position opposite the vicar. "It is time to take this conversation inside. After this lovely concert, it would not do to cause Margherita any more embarrassment."

Luca whirled, his expression stricken.

Margherita reached for him, needing to reassure him. Her bad leg caught on the stool. Signore Ferryman tried to snag her waist, but Margherita's forward momentum sent her to the ground with a cry.

Only, she landed in Luca's arms. Again.

He was on his knees, she lying across his lap. He pressed a kiss to her temple and whispered, "I will always catch you."

Paulo's laugh shattered the moment.

Margherita buried her face in Luca's chest. Was this the end of her time in Eden Cove?

"Luca, bring Margherita to St. Bartholomew's. We will finish this conversation there." Constable Bailey helped Luca and Margherita to their feet, then to the crowd, he added, "The rest of you, go home before I begin writing up charges."

"But we deserve to know who the Ferrymans have been harboring." An elegant woman rose from the very back row.

"Miss Walker?" Luca stared.

"Yeah, who is this musician?" Another person demanded.

"We need to know."

"Tell us!"

Paulo smirked.

"Bailey, we can't hide this," Luca said. "I think we tell them everything. That is, Margherita, if you are agreeable?"

Margherita leaned into Luca, trying to force her tongue to speak English.

"You can stay right here at my side." Luca held her closer.

Paulo muttered something lascivious in Italian and embarrassment flooded her. She needed to be free of him. Defeat him. Because he would not stop until she was destroyed.

"Sì, sì, Luca."

Luca nodded to Constable Bailey, and the man insisted Signore and Signora Ferryman, as well as the vicar, return to their seats. They protested, of course, but Constable Bailey refused to reconsider. While he did not say as much, Margherita had the feeling he desired only the accused and accuser to stand before the town. And if Margherita hadn't been clinging to Luca, he probably would have made Luca sit, too.

Mamma mia. How had they gotten here? The happy moments before the earthquake were nothing but rubble. "Why do you hate me so?" she asked Paulo in Italian as the constable instructed everyone to sit.

Paulo sneered, keeping to Italian so no one would understand them. "Because you are alive. Earthquake, fire, escape across the water ... you are a witch who will not die. Worse, you have an imperfection that must be eradicated from this earth. The thought of your offspring disgusts me."

If he'd carved out her heart, his words would not hurt less. She buried her face in Luca's arm, Paulo's chuckling echoing in her ears.

"Don't listen to him." Luke spoke so softly. "He means to wound you."

"He has." Somehow, she found the English words.

"I know, which is why this needs to end." He kissed her hair. "Mi dispiace."

"Oh Luca."

Constable Bailey cleared his throat. "I do not approve of this, however I acknowledge the people of Eden Cove want to know the truth. One such resident has already approached me, suggesting Margherita is here illegally."

"Who?" Luca demanded as people murmured.

Pieces snapped together. "Signora Archer?" Margherita asked.

Constable Bailey gave a subtle nod, and Luca muttered something about a new housekeeper.

"I will take her away from here so your people need not fear her." Again, Paulo spoke loud enough for the entire crowd to hear.

Luca opened his mouth, likely to refute the statement, considering the fury quivering the muscles of the arm that held her, but Margherita hushed him. Paulo would keep spouting anything against her and Luca's defense only hindered them from laying the truth before the people. This was her trial. The town her judges.

Constable Bailey motioned for the crowd to quiet. "When this concerned citizen approached me, I recognized the subject as the foreigner who was in the bakery at the time of the fire."

"You survived another fire?" Paulo could have been a fire-breather for the hate that spewed from him.

"Please keep your comments to yourself." Constable Bailey glared at Paulo, then softened his expression for the townspeople. "I am here to assure you that I have investigated all week. Miss Margherita Vicienzo did not start the fire that exploded in the bakery."

Paulo's bluster, the townspeople's excited chatter, it all drowned out Margherita's own relieved sigh.

Luca tightened his hold on her and whispered against her hair, "Don't relax yet."

It took her a moment to realize Constable Bailey said nothing about her illegal status.

"But she is here illegally, isn't she?" Someone called from the crowd. Margherita guessed either Signora Archer or Alice Walker.

"This is correct." Paulo jumped on the opportunity. "I know she is here illegally."

"Paulo, no." Margherita tried to stop him, even though she knew it was hopeless. The crowd erupted. Shouts. Accusations. It swarmed around her, threatening to drown her. Oh, why would God not make it stop?

"Wait!" Luca threw up a hand, silencing everyone in an instant. He looked to Reverend Charles. "What would it require to marry Margherita?"

A squeak jumped from Margherita's throat, but she doubted anyone had heard over Paulo's explosion of words.

Constable Bailey blew his whistle. "The question should be put to Margherita first, should it not? However, Luke, if you are offering to marry her merely to allow her to stay in the country, that is not good enough."

Margherita squeezed her eyes closed. Her life rested on his answer.

Luca wrapped his other arm around her, pressing her head against his chest. "I won't let this brute take her back to Italy and murder her."

"She is a witch." Paulo shouted back. "She killed my sister."

Oh, why could she not hide? To have this conversation before the entire town of Eden Cove. If Luca did not hold her up, she would sink into the ground.

Constable Bailey blew his whistle again.

"You are mistaken, Mr. Sorrentino." Reverend Charles joined them. "Margherita was a victim in the earthquake that collapsed the building around Margherita and Maria."

"How do you know my sister's name?" Paulo's volume grew louder, if that were possible. It echoed in Margherita's chest, like the crashing of the stones that killed her friend. She trembled, and Luca held her close.

"That is not the question." Bailey's tone had Margherita raising her head. He didn't wonder at Paulo's accusation? "Margherita, I wish to know whether you have any interest in marrying Luke Ferryman?"

"Interest?" The word confused her. His tone baffled her. She looked from the constable to the vicar to Paulo. Without these witnesses, she had no doubt, Paulo would put a violent end to this conversation. To her.

Luca slid his arms from around her, his hands running down her arms so that he never let her go. The action drew her attention away from Paulo. How did Luca know just how to clasp her hands to aid her balance?

"Margherita?" Luca's thumbs traced her knuckles and the surrounding sounds faded. "Could you love me someday?"

Margherita opened her mouth, closed it. "Do you ..." She couldn't think of the English way to ask her question.

Luke lowered to one knee, never taking his eyes from hers. "Do I love you? Yes, Margherita. I love you. I admire you and think you're the bravest, strongest, most beautiful woman I have ever met. As I sat there, listening to your music, I could not fathom a world where you could love me. Where I would be worthy of you. Is there any hope of it?"

Oh, blessed man. This was nothing like Paulo's proposal. For all his bluster, he lacked the emotion Luca showed her. The deep quiet that kept her safe as a storm raged around them. Her knees buckled and in an instant, Luca stood with her in his arms. Safe, safe arms.

"Sì, sì." Tears clogged her voice and she bobbed her head. She could not let him wait or wonder. "*Ti amo*, Luca. *Ti amo moltissimo.*"

The crowd cheered. Cheered! But Luca bent close. "I don't know what you said, but I hope it means you love me, too."

Margherita gave a watery laugh. "Si, Luca. I love you very—"

A man's roar stopped her words. The next instant, Paulo took her and Luca to the ground.

Chapter Thirteen

MARGHERITA GASPED FOR BREATH as Luca and Paulo both landed atop her. The next instant, Luca had shoved Paulo aside and rolled off of her. Paulo recovered quickly and launched himself at Luca again. Margherita scrambled out of their way as Constable Bailey's whistle blew.

Signora Ferryman pulled Margherita a safe distance away. While Margherita gathered herself, Signore Ferryman hauled Luca to his feet while two men held Paulo by the arms.

Constable Bailey glared at her former fiancé. "Mr. Sorrentino, how did you get into this country?"

Paulo, face red as a tomato, looked like Mount Vesuvius about to spew its lava.

Luca glanced about, relief sagging his shoulders when he spotted Margherita. Signora Ferryman relinquished her to him.

Luca wrapped Margherita close and Margherita clung to him. Neither said a word—no words were needed—as they watched Bailey transform from a mild-mannered constable to an intense detective.

He wagged a finger in Paulo's face. "See, I think Mrs. Archer was onto something when she brought her concerns to me. I ask again, how did you get into this country?"

Paulo bared clenched teeth.

"As you wish." Constable Bailey motioned to two other men waiting nearby. "Mr. Paulo Sorrentino. You are under arrest for espionage."

Margherita gasped, as did everyone else around her. Paulo's volcano erupted in Italian words that burned her ears. Luke pressed her head against his chest.

"Enough!" Bailey silenced Paulo for a moment. "I understand the Home Office would like a word. These nice gentlemen will escort you."

It took four men to wrestle Paulo into submission, but once that was done and her former fiance had been led away, Constable Bailey apologized to the crowd and waved the vicar to the front.

Reverend Charles motioned for the townspeople's silence. "This was not the ending we hoped for this evening. The collection for the bakery has not yet begun. Consider now, in your offer to help, that Luke is preparing to bring a wife into his home."

The atmosphere lifted at that reminder. Such joyous news washed away the red pallor that Paulo had brought with him. Luca kissed her hair and Margherita felt herself relaxing, her vision clearing.

She sought her mandolin. Had it survived? She hadn't given it a thought in the past minutes. Ah, there it was. Someone had moved it off to the side by her satchel. *Grazie, Signore,* she thanked the Lord. It would have devastated her to lose her most treasured family heirloom, especially after it had made the trip with her from San Mirra.

Reverend Charles waved her and Luca forward. "At this time, I would like to formally request that if anyone has an objection to the marriage of Luke Ferryman to Margherita Vicienzo, please speak now."

Now? Luca's heart pounded beneath Margherita's ear. Or was that her own pulse?

They watched whispers spread through the crowd. And then one woman stood. Signora Archer. "I do."

Behind them, Signora Ferryman muttered less than flattering words about their housekeeper. Sacked housekeeper.

"Don't worry," Luca whispered. How he thought that possible, she didn't know.

Reverend Charles sighed. "What is your concern, Mrs. Archer?"

"She brought that madman here." The older woman waved toward where the men had led Paulo away. "She is a foreigner.

I ask you: how could the only son of the Ferrymans marry a woman who is not British?"

"A valid question." Reverend Charles turned to Luca. "Care to offer your response?"

Luca's shoulders drew back, confidence straightening his spine. His hair might be splayed every which way, his clothing rumpled, dusty, and torn from Paulo's attack, but he looked every bit a leader in this town. And Margherita admired him for it.

"You all know Gran has been matchmaking for years," Luca said, drawing a chuckle from the crowd. "However, I resisted because marrying for duty has never appealed. No, I have longed to marry a woman who I loved the way Grandad loves Gran. The way my late father loved my late mother, God bless them."

"God bless them," the crowd murmured with him.

"How can I marry Margherita? It's simple. I love her. Please, grant me this."

"You have my approval!" someone called out.

"Aye!" said another.

"Kiss her!" shouted someone else and Margherita's cheeks heated.

Reverend Charles raised an eyebrow. "Care to withdraw your objection, Mrs. Archer?"

The poor woman had no choice in the face of the overwhelming support the rest of the townspeople gave Luca. And Margherita. Where her own neighbors had turned on her, called her a witch, and drove her from her home, here these strangers welcomed her with arms open, all because one of their own loved her.

"Wonderful." Reverend Charles gave Signora Archer a look of approval, then grinned at Luca and Margherita. "Who else is looking forward to a Ferryman wedding? In the very near future, I'm sure."

Cheers, hoots, and hollers had Luca's chest bouncing with laughter. Margherita didn't bother burying her smile.

Constable Bailey cleared his throat, kept his voice low. "I do need a word with you both."

Her happiness dimmed, but Reverend Charles kept a cheery smile, likely so no one else suspected the conversation. "Allow me to oversee the collection and clean up. Would you escort Luke and Margherita to my office once they have finished receiving the well-wishers?"

Not given a choice, nor answers to their questions, Margherita and Luca stood beside the collection plate as members of Eden Cove expressed their congratulations and overflowed the collection with their generous donations toward rebuilding the bakery.

Night had fallen when Margherita entered St. Bartholomew's behind Reverend Charles, Luca at her side, Constable Bailey behind them. Their footsteps echoed in the cavernous place. With Paulo's vitriol still ringing in her ears, the stained glass windows brought to mind her last night in her hometown of San Mirra, huddled beneath a window depicting Jesus and the little children.

Jesus had heard her that night. No, He hadn't physically healed her, but he had healed her heart. He had brought her to a man who loved her, who would protect her, and to a town she could call her home.

"Sir, I must ask what this is about." Luca stayed close to her side as they settled in a tight group of chairs in Reverend Charles's office. "It is late and I would like to escort Margherita home."

"And then you will be staying with me until the wedding." Reverend Charles's expression gave no room for disobedience.

"No." Margherita touched Luca's arm. "I cannot push you out of your home. I will go somewhere else."

"It is your home, too." Luca smiled at her, a love shining in his eyes that she had never seen in Paulo. "I will happily leave for the sake of propriety. We'll be together soon enough."

Her stomach fluttered.

"You were right, Reverend." Constable Bailey laughed. "This is a love match. Too syrupy for my taste, but it answers all my concerns."

"Wait. Your concerns?" Luca redirected his attention to the other men.

Margherita began putting pieces together. The fact that Bailey had not arrested her after the oven exploded, nor even insisted on questioning her. Frankly, when he did get around to asking her about the fire, he never made her feel as if she were under investigation. Never once had he pressed her for sensitive information.

She leaned toward him. "You knew I'd been smuggled into the country. Why didn't you do anything about it?"

"She's a smart one, Luke." Bailey withdrew a folded packet from his inner coat pocket. "Yes, I knew you'd been smuggled into the country because I'm the one who provided you with the false paperwork."

"What?" Luca looked from one to the other of them.

Bailey handed her the papers. "And now you are no longer here illegally."

Luca laid his arm over her shoulder as Margherita flipped through the documents. Official documents that meant she no longer needed to hide in fear of being sent back to Italy. "Thank you." The words whooshed out, in English, no less.

"Yes, thank you, constable," Luca shook his head. "But perhaps you ought to start at the beginning? How did this come about?"

"Quite right." Constable Bailey waved at Reverend Charles. "The story begins with you, does it not?"

"No." Reverend Charles pointed a finger at the constable. "You arrived in Eden Cove and gave me the idea."

"Gentlemen," Luke muttered.

Margherita chuckled. She couldn't help it. Bailey's news opened a world of possibility to her.

"Ah, I suppose one side of the thread begins with me." Bailey shrugged. "Before I begin, I ask you to keep this confidential. I am from the Home Office and tonight concludes my investigation into a smuggling ring happening in the area. I leave tomorrow and the new, permanent, and actual constable will be arriving."

Luca's brows reached his hairline. "You're not a constable?"

"No. Just playing the part."

"When Father Benedict told me of your plight, Margherita, I could not sit idly by," Reverend Charles continued the story. "I have contacts in the Home Office, and when the information coincided with Bailey's investigation, it gave us the opportunity to use the smuggling channels in place."

"You used her?" Luca scowled.

"No." Margherita patted his arm, though she enjoyed seeing this emotional side of her usually staid baker and ferryman. "No, they did not use me. They used the criminals to rescue me. I believe I was the thread they could follow to find where the ethics of the underground ended and illegal smuggling began."

"We could use a mind like yours in the Home Office." Bailey chuckled. "Our plan worked. However, it also caused trouble. The boat captain that brought Margherita here recognized Luke, thought he would be a good way to get a foot in town. When Luke rebuffed Miss Walker, she took more drastic means to demand cooperation."

"Alice Walker is a smuggler?" Luke tapped his fingers on Margherita's shoulder. Her uninjured shoulder. "I suspected as much. Why did she want the bakery?"

Constable Bailey shifted in his chair. "She wanted to use it as a drop point. No one would question middle of the night deliveries and you would be a ferryman, eventually."

"I wasn't going to sell," Luca said.

Bailey shrugged. "She figured that out quickly."

Margherita chewed her lip, working up her courage until she could ask, "Did she blow up the oven?" Luca shifted closer to her; dear man, to notice her discomfort over the question.

Bailey scratched one of his sideburns. "I suspect so, though I have no proof. We won't know until we question her. My men are picking her up—quietly—because we need her to help us find the ship captain who brought Margherita to Eden Cove. It appears she told him about Margherita and the captain sent word to Paulo."

"That is how he found me?" Margherita shuddered.

Luca covered her clenched hands with his rough one. "The captain is still at large?"

"Not for long." Bailey sounded sure. "We'll have this smuggling ring wrapped up. They made a grave error setting Paulo loose in Eden Cove."

"Okay." Luca squeezed her hands. "But I feel like there is still a piece missing."

"That would be my side of the story." Reverend Charles spoke up with a smile. "You forget, Luke, that I have known you your whole life. I also knew much about Margherita. My connections with the Home Office allowed for them to do their due diligence while Margherita made her way here. Couldn't have a spy being smuggled into the country, now, could we?"

"You played matchmaker." Luca rolled his eyes, but they twinkled, too. "And I thought it was my grandmother."

Bailey shook his head without humor. "I couldn't condone a marriage unless I saw something real between you. But Charles insisted it would develop, so I began the paperwork such a marriage would require. Prepared to tear it all up if it didn't turn out the way he thought, too."

Reverend Charles harrumphed. "Prayed, you mean."

"Regardless." Bailey withdrew another packet of papers from his coat pocket. "I'll need your signatures, then I will see this delivered to the registrar's office. Once it's processed, you can marry and live happily ever after. I'll expedite it, so it won't take long. And you don't need to read the banns before then unless you wish. Though you already did the first of the three today, to a rousing affirmation."

"This is all wonderful, but ..." Luke turned to Margherita, sliding his arm from around her shoulders to cup her hands in both of his. "Now that we have less of an audience, and you've heard the machinations behind the scenes, Margherita, do you still want to marry? And marry quickly? Please be honest with me."

Dear, dear man. He would sacrifice for her, she had no doubt of that. "You first, Luca. Do you wish to marry me?"

"Absolutely." He spoke before she could give all the reasons he shouldn't want to marry her, the reasons Paulo had turned against her. "I love you, Margherita. Nothing will change my mind, but if you ..."

She put a finger on his lips, waiting until he fell silent before she said. "I only want to make sure you want to marry me. Now that you have heard the *macchinazioni*." She couldn't help tossing in a bit of Italian, happiness growing like the first notes of a new song.

"I want nothing more." Luke clasped her wrist to remove her finger from his lips, then leaned forward to kiss her.

"In a church, Ferryman?" Bailey grumbled.

Luke paused an inch away from her and tilted his head. "I plan to pledge my love for this woman before God and man, why not kiss her before Him, too?"

Margherita laughed, her joy complete. "*Ti amerò per sempre, Luca.*"

Luke gave her a quick kiss. "And that means?"

"I love you forever."

"Ti amerò per sempre, Margherita." And he kissed her again.

Saturday, 24 October, 1931
Bella Matrone
Crow's Nest, Wisconsin
United States of America

Dearest Bella,

I am giddy and unable to sleep. Tomorrow I become Mrs. Luke Ferryman!

The past two months have been some of the hardest I have faced, and yet they have brought me to Luca and Eden Cove. I am happy here, Bella. God knew. I am glad I trusted Him. Though some days I thought I would see Him face-to-face before my prayers ended.

I desire to put some of those days behind me. Paulo is gone from my life. No longer can he wield hate and fear. I refuse to dwell on the pain he caused. My life must move forward into the blessing God has given me. Tomorrow begins a new day.

But do say a prayer for Italia, Bella, that God will have mercy and good will triumph. I fear what the future will bring for our homeland.

The grandfather clock downstairs is chiming midnight. It is my wedding day. I must try to sleep.

Si, si, I hear your request to hear all about the wedding. It will be in Luca's church and I will wear Signora Ferryman's white gown. It is lacey and gorgeous. Of course, I am much shorter and smaller, so we had to tailor it. And Luca will wear a black suit. How handsome he will look!

I can hear your nonna reminding us girls that marriage is sacred, but it is not easy. Remember how we would dream of our future husbands? Luca was not the one I pictured, but he is wonderful. God knew, Bella. If you are to marry someday, God knows that, too.

I hope you have received my letters. I miss your words.

Margherita

Read on for …
The Ferryman Family Scone Recipe
An Italian-English Glossary
And an excerpt from
The Outsider's Welcome
2 Sycamore Street
Then download a Bonus Letter from Bella to Margherita

From the Author

Dear Reader,

Thank you for reading Luke and Margherita's story. I hope you enjoyed their romance.

If Margherita's letters to Bella intrigued you, I invite you to visit Crow's Nest, in *Confessions to a Stranger*, where danger and romance meet at the water's edge. Find out more at daniellegrandinetti.com/confessions-to-a-stranger.

Special thanks to Anna Jenson for inviting me to be a part of the Our House on Sycamore series. Little did I know when I picked 1 Sycamore that Luke was part of such a multi-generational family. As you read the rest of the series, you'll see what I mean! This is my first foray in writing a story outside of the United States, and I greatly enjoyed working with authors from across the globe. I hope you'll love their stories, too!

Thank you, too, to Ann Elizabeth Fryer, Sarah Hinkle, and my proofreaders for making this story shine.

To Roseanna White and her Patrons and Peers group who helped me talk through the ethical and spiritual challenges Luke, in particular, battled in this story. Much of their wisdom and insight filtered into the pages.

And last, but certainly not least, a great big thank you to my husband and boys for giving me the time to turn these thoughts into a story for you.

It's been a delight to see this story become a reality. If you've enjoyed *The Italian Musician's Sanctuary*, I'd be most grateful if you'd take a moment to leave an honest review. And don't miss the bonus letter from Bella! You'll find the link after the chapter from *The Outsider's Welcome* by Vida Li Sik.

Thank you, again, for joining me for Luke and Margherita's story. To keep in touch, find me at daniellegrandinetti.com.

Happy reading!

Danielle Grandinetti

Ferryman Scone Recipe

The famed Ferryman scone recipe is based on an old recipe from one of the popular baking companies. However, not only am I Italian, which means I can never follow a recipe, I adapted this one to work with 1930s ingredients.

A special thanks to my sister who helped me bake a trial batch and to our husbands and children who happily declared them a success. Here's the recipe as we made it, but feel free to adapt as you see fit!

For example, dates and raisins would have been available dried fruit in the 1930s, but you could use dried cranberries or blueberries, or any dried fruit you'd like to try.

As this story tells, there are different types of oranges and their availability ebbed and flowed with the economic times and the advent of war. We used a clementine in our trial batch because it was the type of orange we had on hand.

Baking powder has a fascinating history, as the story also alludes to. Fortunately, the baking powder we have today is the same they would have used in 1930. To find out more, check out the article, "The Great Uprising: How a Powder Revolutionized Baking" by Ben Panko, from *The Smithsonian Magazine*, dated June 20, 2017.

Powdered sugar was one of the ingredients Luke and Margherita would not have had in 1930. However it is merely a mixture of cornstarch and white sugar. To make this recipe 1930s authentic, we made our own powdered sugar, and included the measurements in the recipe.

One last note, though this story takes place in England, I used US measurements.

I hope you enjoy this 1930s scone recipe!

Ferryman Family Scones

1. In large bowl, mix the following (may be set aside until the next day):

    a. 2 cups flour

    b. 3 tablespoons sugar

    c. 3 teaspoons baking powder

    d. 2 teaspoons grated orange peel

    e. 1/2 teaspoon salt

2. Preheat oven to 400 degrees Fahrenheit and grease cookie sheet using a stick of butter

3. When ready to bake, pour the following into the dry ingredients, and mix only until moist:

   a. 1/2 tsp vanilla

   b. 1/2 cup chopped dates

   c. 1/4 cup raisins

   d. 1 1/3 cups whipping cream

4. On lightly floured surface, knead dough until smooth (6-7 times). Divide dough in half to create two rounds of approximately 1-1 1/2 inches in thickness. Cut rounds into quarters and place wedges on greased cookie sheet. Bake for 13 minutes or until light golden brown.

5. While wedges cool, mix the following ingredients into a glaze:

   a. 1c corn starch

   b. 1c sugar

   c. Juice from an orange until at proper glaze

constancy

6. Drizzle glaze over wedges and serve warm.

Italian-English Glossary

Abbi pieta – have mercy

Aiuto – help

Arancia rossa – red orange

Arrivederci – goodbye

Artista – artist

Bagno – bathroom/loo

Brutta – ugly

Caffe – coffee

Che – what

Cucina – kitchen

Diavola – devil

Dio – God

Donna – woman/lady

Fidanzato – fiancé

Formaggio – cheese

Grazie – thank you

Incapace – unable

Inadatta – unfit

Inghilterra – England

Inutile – useless

Italiano – Italian

Ite in pace – go in peace

La mia bambina – my child

Macchinazioni – machinations

Mamma mia – an exclamation

Mi dispiace – I'm sorry

Molto bello/bella – very beautiful

Molto bene – very good

Musicista – musician

Nonno/nonna/nonni – grandfather/mother/parents

Padre – father

Panino – sandwich

Pasticcino – pastry

Per favore – please

Polizia – police

Qui micio, micio – here kitty, kitty

Resistenza – resistance

Riproduzione – reproduction

Salvatore – savior

Scusa – excuse me

Senza valore – worthless

Sfogliatella – an Italian dessert

Si – yes

Signore/signora – Mister/missus

Spirto Santo – Holy Spirit

Strega – witch

Ti amerò per sempre – I love you forever

Ti amo moltissimo – I love you very much

Traghettatrice – ferrywoman

Tu perisci – you die

Veniere – come

Enjoy a sneak peek of...

The
OUTSIDER'S
WELCOME

Vida Li Sik

IMKA WRINKLED HER NOSE at the pungent smell of exhaust fumes from passing cars and expelled a breath of air that dissipated in a vapor-like cloud under the shy sun.

Everything was unfamiliar to her—the weather, trees, busyness, myriads of accents, and the standoffish people in the capital. She lifted her chin. But she'd get used to it. New beginnings were difficult. Granny Margaret assured her people were friendlier the farther you moved from London. Life in Eden Cove should be safer. That was Imka's primary concern.

They turned into a street dotted with several little shops. Dan looked at her over Charlie's head. "Where would you like to go for lunch?"

Imka didn't hesitate. "Let's go to Harry's Fish and Chips. It's child-friendly."

He chuckled. "Ah. So, you're sacrificing for Charlie. Right?"

She punched him lightly on the arm. "Of course. Tell me the aroma of fish and hot chips isn't intoxicating." Their noses led them to the cafe. Imka licked her lips in anticipation.

The doorbell tinkled when they stepped inside. A broad smile split the leathery face of the man behind the counter. "My customers from South Africa. Your usual table?"

At Dan's nod, he picked up the highchair in front of the counter and led them to a corner where one table was slightly apart from the rest—perfect for a couple with a toddler in tow.

Dan settled Charlie into her seat, engaging in a mini battle while he strapped her in. When she slid into the plastic chair, Imka scanned the room. There were only a few other customers in the shop, with the Louws the only ones who opted to sit. Imka and Mr Patel exchanged names on the first day they'd walked into his little restaurant. The owner now waited with two menus in hand. He smiled at Charlie but addressed her. "What can I get you today?"

Imka didn't need to look at the menu, she knew what she wanted. She smiled at Mr Patel. "A pot of tea for me. Fish nuggets and chips for the little lady. I'll have that lovely, battered fish you make with hot chips drowned in vinegar. Just for a change."

"Just for a change, huh." Dan grinned. He took off his beanie and added his order. "I'll have the same, minus the vinegar."

Mr Patel's head bobbed. He pointed at the skully with the logo of Dan's new employers. "When do you leave for the North Sea?" The friendly man had extracted their life history and plans on the first night they walked into his restaurant.

Dan touched the knitted cap, a small smile playing on his lips. "A week from now. I've got to help Imka and Charlie settle in first. Then it's off to Aberdeen, and a flight from there to the rig."

"Exciting times." Mr Patel's eyes twinkled with curiosity. "You know, when you first came in here and told me about working as an electrical technician on an oil rig, I thought, 'here's a man who doesn't shy away from adventure.'"

Dan chuckled, glancing at Imka. "Well, it's a big change, but we're ready for it."

"Imka, how about you?" The shop owner's tone was gentle. "What will you do while Dan's away?"

She swallowed and stroked her baby bump. "I'll look after Charlie. Maybe find a nursery school for her and a new job for me." Imka clenched her hands together on her lap, but schooled her face into a mask of confidence she didn't feel. Her future loomed as an uncertain mist on the horizon, but she was determined to make it work. The move had to be for the best—for Dan, for her, and their daughter. Once they decided to relocate to England, Imka committed fully. She would channel all her energy into transforming Granny's house into a home for them.

Imka leant back in her seat so that Mr Patel could place a teapot and cups on the table. Once he left, she poured a cup for Dan and herself.

"Tea. Tea." Charlie squealed, banging a teaspoon on the highchair's tray. Her gaze flitted between her parents. She was a carbon copy of her dad with her light hair and green eyes, but she had inherited Imka's snub nose and high cheekbones.

She touched her daughter's hand to still the banging noise. "Yours is coming, Charlie. Patience, my girl." With an indulgent smile, Imka twisted to take out a glass cup filled with black

Rooibos tea from the baby bag on the seat next to her. A sharp pain lanced through her groin area when she straightened up. She grimaced.

"Are you okay?" Dan didn't miss anything. Sometimes she wished he wouldn't fuss over her so much. Even if it came from a place of love. He'd been a reassuring anchor throughout their four years of marriage.

She placed the cup in front of Charlie who grabbed and slurped from it. "Ja. I'm okay. It was just a twinge."

He covered her hand; his long fingers oozed warmth and comfort. He'd always affected her so. One of the reasons she loved him so much. Well, that and his lean, toned physique, mop of dirty blond hair, and green eyes.

"Should we find a doctor?" Concerned etched itself around his mouth.

She was quick to reassure him. "No. It's probably normal. Every pregnancy's different, and this baby's finding space."

His raised eyebrow said it all. Her second pregnancy wasn't as easy as her first. But she'd manage. He took a sip from his tea and sighed. "Your instincts are right most of the time. But, if you're ever in doubt, promise you'll call the doctor."

She flashed a grateful smile and mimed a scout's salute. "Scout's honour. How 'bout you? Are you ready for your adventure at sea?"

He twined his fingers around hers. "Only because I have you to come home to. Today's sermon hit home for me. I can relate to Abram and Sarah who left everything they knew behind. We chose to leave South Africa, so it's different, but the essence is the same. Just like them, we've ventured into an unfamiliar place, relying on each other to make it our own."

"I feel the same. Although Eden Cove isn't entirely unfamiliar to you. You've visited Granny Margaret in the past."

He nodded. "But visiting and living in an area are two different things. Life in a village is very different from that in the city. And you'll be the one to deal with the busybodies while I'm gone. Granny is happy to be away from them. She's enjoying her trip around the world."

Like a swallow, his granny chased after the sun during the northern hemisphere winter and enjoyed the moderate temperatures in South Africa. They'd accompanied her to Durban where she'd boarded the first cruise ship, with plans to see her again when she returned to Eden Cove.

"It's a welcome distraction after the loss of your grandfather. I can imagine Betty will keep her busy wherever they go," she said.

He nodded. "And you? Are you ready to feather your new nest?"

His granny offered them her house and hinted she might move in with Betty— her younger sister who was also her best friend— on her return. Her spinster sister's house in Somerby would easily accommodate the two of them. She said living in

Eden Cove without her husband had become too painful and gave them freedom to make whatever changes they wanted.

"Of course. Luckily, we won't be starting from scratch. I won't disturb your granny's eclectic furnishings even though we have her approval to change things up. Except for adding an electric fence, of course."

Dan paused, his hand halfway to his mouth. He put down his cup. A frown creased his brow. "About that. You remember Granny said we'd need to first get permission? She said the neighbours reluctantly agreed to the palisade fence I put up last year. They might not welcome further modifications. We'll have to talk to them again."

Irritation flooded her chest, making her hot and cold at the same time. "Well, your gran refused to be bullied, and so will we." She pulled on her hand, but he tightened his fingers, unwilling to let go.

His gaze was steady and calm. "It's something we'll have to navigate carefully. The last thing we want is start off on the wrong foot in the community."

She bit back an angry retort. "Agreed. But we also need to stand our ground if necessary. We can't allow them to push us around."

He squeezed her fingers, and they shared a determined glance. The reality of the challenges ahead settled between them, a silent promise to face whatever came their way together.

Continue reading in
The Outsider's Welcome
Visit vidalisik.com.

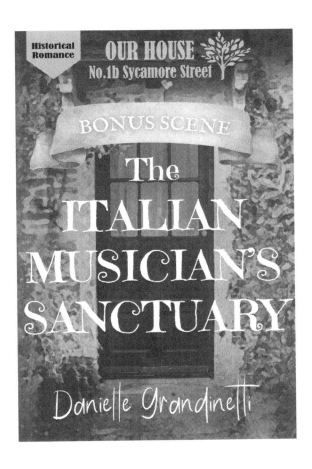

Read Bella's Bonus Letter at:
daniellegrandinetti.com/letter-from-bella
Use code FromBella

OUR HOUSE on Sycamore Street

BOOK 1: THE FERRYMAN'S LIGHT   *by Anna Jensen*

He has plans for the future. What happens when circumstances dictate those plans must change?

BOOK 2: THE ITALIAN MUSICIAN'S SANCTUARY
by Danielle Grandinetti

Hunted by one man, can she open her heart to another?

BOOK 3: THE OUTSIDER'S WELCOME
by Vida Li Sik

If you love women's fiction, you will enjoy The Outsider's Welcome, a tale of resilience, community, and a search for belonging.

BOOK 4: THE DAUGHTER'S TRUTH *by Claire Lagerwall*

Emmy Whitehouse is about to discover that everything she knows is not at all what she thinks.

BOOK 5: THE LIGHT KEEPER'S WIFE
by Jennifer Mistmorgan

They've come to escape their wartime secrets. But are some shadows too dark to shake off?

BOOK 6: THE KEY COLLECTOR'S PROMISE
by Donna Jo Stone

She came to warn her estranged mother of danger. But will the cost of unraveling family secrets be too much to bear?

BOOK 7: THE MAESTRO'S MISSING MELODY
by Amy Walsh

She is thrilled to apprentice with her fiddler hero—until his grumpiness knocks him off his pedestal.

BOOK 8: THE NIECE'S AUSSIE PATIENT
by Meredith Resce

Newly graduated in hospitality management, Stephanie Delafonte is looking forward to managing her aunt's guest house for three weeks while Lina takes a well-earned break.

BOOK 9: THE RUNAWAY'S REDEMPTION
by Allyson Koekhoven

A tragic event at work leaves South African paramedic Johlene Anderson reeling.

BOOK 10: THE BOOKBINDER'S DAUGHTER
by Lynn Dean

A war refugee is invited to live with an aging recluse but learns too late she's being used.

BOOK 11: THE WIDOW'S REQUEST *by Ashley Winter*

Join Fiona as she unravels old family secrets, faces danger head on and uncovers the truth about her parents' deception...

BOOK 12: THE LOST DAUGHTER'S IRISHMAN

by Carolyn Miller

She wants to find a way to live again; he wants to close a deal and move on. Until sparks fly and these opposites attract in this contemporary romance filled with heart and humour.

BOOK 13: THE MOTHER'S SONG *by Caroline Johnston*

Miranda McVitty, wife, mother and campsite owner. Miranda loves to sing as she goes about her work and this summer she's learning to sing her prayers as well as her to do list.

BOOK 14: THE WEDDING PLANNER'S PREDICAMENT

by Dianne J. Wilson

Cleo is done organizing weddings. James has a wedding to plan, and Cleo is his only hope.

Harbored in Crow's Nest

Welcome to Crow's Nest,
where danger and romance meet at the water's edge.
daniellegrandinetti.com/harbored-in-crows-nest

Confessions to a Stranger

Harbored in Crow's Nest, #1

**She's lost her future. He's sacrificed his.
Now they have a chance to reclaim it—together.**

Refuge for the Archaeologist

Harbored in Crow's Nest, #2

**Will uncovering the truth set them free
or destroy what they hold most dear?**

Escape with the Prodigal

Harbored in Crow's Nest, #3

**Only a Christmas miracle will save
an unwed mother and the lumberjack protecting her.**

Relying on the Enemy

Harbored in Crow's Nest, #4

**She's protecting her children.
He's redeeming his past.**

Sheltered by the Doctor

Harbored in Crow's Nest, #5

**A fake relationship might keep her safe,
but will it break their hearts?**

Investigation of a Journalist

Harbored in Crow's Nest, #6

**A second chance to set the record straight,
and rekindle a lost love.**